"Stop looking at me like that." His low growl rumbled over the silent courtyard.

"How am I looking at you?" Nikhat said, tucking her feet beneath her legs.

Azeez leant his head back, giving her a perfect view of the strong column of his neck. Even dressed in the most casual clothes, he epitomized the supreme male arrogance and confidence that had always messed with her usually practical personality. And continued to do so, if she was ready to admit the truth.

"Like you cannot stop. Like you want to eat me up alive."

The heat rising through her cheeks had nothing to do with the sun. "That's not true."

He leaned forward, his gaze thoughtful. "Yes, it is. There's a temerity in your gaze now. You always knew your own mind, but now it's like your body has caught up."

She shrugged, holding herself tight and still under his scrutiny. The look Azeez cast in her direction was thorough. "I'm not a shy twenty-two-year-old anymore."

"I can see that." A lick of something came alive in his gaze. "I can almost see you staring down your patients into good health."

Nikhat laughed, half to hide the little tremble that went through her. "I do have a reputation as the scary doctor. If only things could be fixed so simply. And you're right. I can't stop looking at you. I can't stop wondering what in Allah's name you think you're doing to yourself."

A DYNASTY
OF SAND AND SCANDAL

A throne where secrets never sleep!

The Desert Kingdom of Dahaar has been beset by tragedy, scandal and secrets for as long as anyone can remember.

Those that reach for the crown are forced to pay a high price indeed. When duty calls, these royals *must* obey…

But these are children of the desert,
and the fires of passion run hot in their veins.

And rarely does passion pair with duty.

Have you read the first title in this unstoppable miniseries by author Tara Pammi?

THE LAST PRINCE OF DAHAAR

This month read:

THE TRUE KING OF DAHAAR

THE TRUE KING OF DAHAAR

BY
TARA PAMMI

First published in Great Britain 2014
by Mills & Boon, an imprint of Harlequin (UK) Limited,
Eton House, 18-24 Paradise Road, Richmond, Surrey, TW9 1SR

© 2014 Tara Pammi

ISBN: 978-0-263-24328-4

Harlequin (UK) Limited's policy is to use papers that are natural,
renewable and recyclable products and made from wood grown in
sustainable forests. The logging and manufacturing processes conform
to the legal environmental regulations of the country of origin.

Printed and bound in Great Britain
by CPI Antony Rowe, Chippenham, Wiltshire

Tara Pammi can't remember a moment when she wasn't lost in a book—especially a Mills & Boon® romance, which provided so much more excitement to a teenager than a mathematics textbook. It was only years later, while struggling with her two-hundred-page thesis in a basement lab, that Tara realised what she really wanted to do: write a romance novel. She already had the requirements—a wild imagination and a love for the written word.

Tara lives in Colorado with the most co-operative man on the planet and two daughters. Her husband and daughters are the only things that stand between Tara and a full-blown hermit life with only books for company.

Tara would love to hear from readers. She can be reached at tara.pammi@gmail.com or through her website: www.tarapammi.com

Recent titles by the same author:

A DEAL WITH DEMAKIS
THE LAST PRINCE OF DAHAAR
  (A Dynasty of Sand and Scandal)
A TOUCH OF TEMPTATION
  (The Sensational Stanton sisters)
A HINT OF SCANDAL
  (The Sensational Stanton sisters)

Did you

For my sister and my friend—
you're an inspiration to me, always.

CHAPTER ONE

DR. NIKHAT ZAKHARI followed the uniformed guard through the carpeted corridor of the Dahaaran palace, assaulted from every side by bittersweet memories. Eight years ago she had known every inch of these corridors and halls, every wall and arch. This palace, the royal family, they had all been part of a dream she had weaved as a naive girl of twenty-two.

Before it had come crumbling down upon her and shattered her.

She stepped over the threshold into the office and the guard closed the door behind her. The formal pumps she had chosen instead of her usual Crocs sank into the lush carpet with a sigh.

She had been in this office one night when the Crown Prince had been the man she had loved, the two of them slipping in like thieves in the night.

All because she had voiced a juvenile wish to see it. Her long-sleeved thick silk jacket couldn't dispel the chill that settled on her skin at the memory.

Drawn to the huge portrait of the royal family behind the dark sandalwood desk, she gave in to nostalgia.

King Malik and Queen Fatima, Ayaan and Amira, each member of the royal family was smiling in the picture ex-

cept Azeez. Because of what Nikhat had told him that day
eight years ago.

A cavern of longing opened up inside of her. Even thou-
sands of miles away, she had felt as if she had lost her own
family when she heard of the attack. Her throat ached, her
vision felt dizzy. She ran trembling fingers over Azeez's
face in the photo.

She leaned her head against the wall. Seeing this familiar place without him was shaking the very foundations of
the life she had resolutely built for herself.

And she couldn't—she wouldn't—give that much power
to a memory. Couldn't let it undo everything she had accomplished.

"How have you been, Nikhat?"

She turned around and stared at the new Crown Prince,
Ayaan bin Riyaaz Al-Sharif, the boy she had once tutored
in chemistry. His copper-gold gaze shone with warmth.
The cut of his features, so similar to Azeez's, knocked the
breath out of her.

She had gone into shock the day she had heard of the
terrorist attack. To see Ayaan again, so many years later
filled her with a joy she couldn't contain. Nikhat reached
him, and hugged him.

Something she wouldn't have dared do eight years ear-
lier.

A soft chuckle shook his lean frame. Stepping back,
Nikhat fought the urge to apologize for her impulsive ges-
ture. Her composure was shaken by being back here but not
torn. A woman, and one not connected to the royal family in
any way, would never have hugged the Crown Prince. But
she was not the average Dahaaran woman anymore, bound
by its traditions and customs. "It's good to see you, Ayaan."

He nodded, his gaze studying her with unhidden thoroughness. "You, too, Nikhat."

He led her to the sitting area, where a silver tea service waited. Settling down opposite him, Nikhat shook her head when he inquired if she wanted something.

The Ayaan that she had known had always had a twinkle in his eyes, a core made of pure joy. The Crown Prince that looked at her now had the mantle of Dahaar weighing him down. There was grief in those eyes of his, a hardness that had found a permanent place in his features.

She had been back in the capital city of Dahaara hardly a day before she had been summoned to a private meeting by the Crown Prince. Not something she could have actually refused, even if she had wanted to. "How did you know I was back in Dahaara?" she said, getting straight to the point.

He shrugged and crossed his legs. Hesitation danced in his eyes before he said, "I have an offer for you."

Nikhat frowned. After eight years with no word from her father, she had been beyond thrilled to hear his voice. But now…"You ordered my father to call me home," she said, the unease she had felt the minute she had received his request solidifying. "You knew how eager I would be to see my family. That's a low blow, Your Highness."

Ayaan rubbed his brow, no hint of guilt in his steady gaze. "It's the price I have to pay for that title, Nikhat."

His words were simple, yet the weight of responsibility behind them struck Nikhat. Clamping down her anger, she remained seated. "Fine, you have me here now. I should warn you though. I'm not a genie to automatically grant your wish."

A sudden smile split his mouth, warmth spilling into his eyes. And the flash of another face, smiling like that, similar yet different, rose in front of her eyes.

Her chest felt incredibly tight and she forced herself to breathe through it. There were going to be reminders of

Azeez everywhere in Dahaar. And she refused to spiral into an emotional mess every time she came across one.

She had done that long enough when she had left eight years ago.

"I see that you have not changed at all. Which is good for me."

"No riddles, Ayaan," she said, forcing herself to address him as the young man she once knew.

"How would you like to spearhead a top-notch women's clinic here in Dahaara? You'll have complete authority on its administration. I'll even get the Ministry to sign off on a health-care-worker training program, specifically for women. It is something I have had in mind and you are without a doubt the best candidate for it."

Shock spiraling through her, Nikhat had no words.

All the longing she had held at bay for eight years, the loneliness that had churned through her, rose to the surface. It was what she had wanted when she had begged her father to let her study medicine, her one goal that had become her focus and anchor when everything else had fallen apart, the impossible dream that had pulled her back to Dahaar from a prestigious position in New York.

She had readied herself for an uphill battle against prejudices masquerading as traditions, and so much more. The sound of disbelief ringing through her must have escaped, because Ayaan clasped her hand.

"You can make a home here in Dahaara, Nikhat. Be near your family again," Ayaan continued.

Nikhat nodded, eternally grateful for his understanding. Ayaan had always been the kinder of the two brothers. Whereas Azeez...there had never been any middle ground with him.

She returned his clasp, clinging to the high of his announcement. "It's all I've ever wanted, Ayaan."

A flicker of unease entered his gaze. "There's something I require from you in exchange, however. A personal favor for the royal family."

Nikhat shook her head. "I owe my profession to your father. Without King Malik's aid and support, my father would've never let me finish high school, much less study medicine. I don't need to be manipulated or offered incentives if you need something from me. All you have to do is ask."

Ayaan nodded, but the wariness in his gaze didn't recede. "This position, this is something I want you to have. It's what my father wanted for you when he supported your education. But what I'm about to ask stretches the boundaries of gratitude."

Nikhat nodded, trying to keep the anxiety his words caused from her face.

He sucked in a deep breath. "Azeez is alive, Nikhat."

For a few seconds, the meaning of his words didn't sink in.

It felt as if the world around her had slowed down, waiting for the buzzing in her ears to pass. The tightness in her chest morphed into a fist in her throat as she saw the truth in his eyes. A stormlike shiver swept through Nikhat and she fought to hold herself together, to fight the urge to flee the palace and never look back.

How many times was she going to flee?

She had worked so hard to realize her dream, had waited all these years to see her family again and she couldn't let anyone stop her now. Not even the man she had once loved with every breath in her body.

Letting herself breathe through the panic in her head, she forced calm into her voice. "I haven't heard a word about this."

"Because no one other than a few trusted servants and

my parents know. Until I can be sure that revealing that he's alive doesn't have a negative effect on Dahaar, I have to contain it." His voice shook and Nikhat reached for his hand this time, even as she fought her own alarm.

How could he be alive after all these years? How was he now?

"I found him four months ago in the desert and I still have no idea how he survived or what he did these past six years. He refuses to see our parents, he barely tolerates my visits. The true prince of Dahaar is now my prisoner." Utter desolation spewed into his words. "I have managed to keep it a secret until now. It would crush the people of Dahaar to see him like this. They…"

"They worshipped him, I know." He'd been their golden prince, arrogant but charming, courageous, born to rule his country. And he had loved Dahaar with a passion that had colored everything he had done.

His love, his passion…they were like a desert storm, consuming you, changing you if you came out alive.

"I'd hoped that he would get better, that sooner or later, he would decide to rejoin the living." Powerlessness colored his gaze, his words raw and jittery. "But with each passing day, he…"

Azeez is alive.

The words rang round and round in her head. But with the dizzying of her emotions also came the control she had developed in order to flourish in her career. "Ayaan? What's wrong with him?" she demanded, forgetting propriety.

"He is little more than a breathing corpse. He refuses to talk, he refuses to see a doctor. He's refusing to live… Nikhat, and I can't lose him all over again."

A knot of fear unraveled in her stomach now. "What exactly is this favor that you want to ask me?"

"Spend some time with him."

No. The word rang through her. Shaking her head, she stepped away from Ayaan. "I'm an obstetrician, Ayaan. Not a psychiatrist. There's nothing I can do for him that all your specialists can't."

"He won't let anyone see him. You...you he won't refuse."

She felt brittle now, as if her calm was nothing but a facade, as if she would fracture under it. But she couldn't fall apart, she refused to let pain and powerlessness wreak havoc on her again. "You don't know what your brother will do if he sees me."

"Anything is better than what he is now."

"And what about the price I'll have to pay?" The question escaped her before she knew she had said it.

His head jerking up, he studied her. Nikhat looked away. The air between with them reverberated with questions he didn't ask and she didn't answer.

Ayaan reached her, his jaw tight with determination. There was no grief or comforting famillarity in his face now. He was the man who had come back to life against all odds, the man who fought his demons every day to do his duty by Dahaar.

"Would it be such a high price? All I'm asking for is a few months. I'm running out of options. I have to find something that will pull him from this spiral. Spend some time with him alone in the palace. Talk to him, try anything that might—"

"If word of this gets out, I'll be damned for the rest of my life in Dahaara," she said, only realizing after she spoke that she was even considering the proposition. "That clinic you are baiting me with will be nothing but a sand castle."

"The Crown Princess Zohra is pregnant. She needs someone who will stay in the palace, a dedicated ob-gyn.

And as to any time you spend with Azeez, no one will know you are with him. I give you my word, Nikhat. I will protect your reputation with everything I have. My coronation is in two months. At that time, whatever state he is in, you can walk away from him. No one will stop you."

Two months with a man who would once again plunge her into her darkest fear. Two months revisiting everything she couldn't have, couldn't be. *Ya Allah, no.* "You've no idea what you're asking me to do."

"I was hoping that you would accept my proposition, but I cannot give you a choice, Nikhat. Desperation never leaves you with one. As of this moment, you're either the Crown Prince's guest or prisoner. If I have to lock you with him, I'll…" His words reverberated with a pain she herself was very familiar with. "He's my brother. He was once your friend. We owe it to him."

Her friend? Hysterical laughter bubbled up inside her.

Azeez bin Rashid Al Sharif had never been *just* her friend. He had been her champion, he had been her prince, and he had been the man who had promised to make her every dream come true.

And he had kept each and every one of his promises.

Nikhat sprang to her feet and straightened her shoulders. She met Ayaan's gaze and nodded before she could refuse, before ghosts of the past crippled her courage, before her bitterest fear trampled her sense of duty.

She would do it because she owed it to King Malik for turning a middle-class girl's fantastic dream to be a doctor into reality; she would do it for a childhood friend who had been through hell and survived; but more than anything, she would do it for the man who had once loved her more than anything in the world.

It was not his fault that she wasn't the woman he had

thought her. "I will do it," she whispered, the true consequences of what she had accepted weighing her down.

Strong arms embraced her tightly. "I have to warn you, Nikhat. He's not the man you or I knew. I'm not even sure that man exists anymore."

There she was again, tall, beautiful, graceful.

Like a mirage in the desert, she appeared every day during this time to taunt him, to remind him of everything he was not.

The darkest time of the day when dawn was a mere hour away, when he found himself staring at the rise of another day with nothing but self-loathing to greet it with.

However drunk he got, it was the time the reality of everything he had become, everything he had done, pressed upon Azeez.

He had been the Crown Prince once. Now he was the Crown Prince's prisoner, a fitting punishment for the man responsible for his sister's death, his brother's suffering and so much more.

Just the passing thought was enough to feel the palace walls close around him.

A cold breeze flew in through the wide-open doors to his right. The cold nipped at his bare chest, slowly but silently insinuating itself into his muscles. He would feel the effect of it tomorrow morning. His right hip would be stiff enough to seize up.

But his imagination was stubborn tonight, the moment passed, and he saw her again.

Tonight, she wore a dark brown, long-sleeved kaftan made of simple cotton with leggings of the same color underneath. She had always been simple in real life, too, never allowing him to splurge on her, never allowing him anything he had wanted to do with her, for that matter.

Like kiss her, or touch her or possess her.

And yet, he had been her slave.

Her hair, a silky mass of dark brown, was tied back into a high ponytail in the no-nonsense way she had liked. Leaving her golden skin pulled tightly over her features.

A high forehead that had always bothered her—a symbol of her intelligence—almond-shaped copper-hued eyes, which were her best feature, her too-long nose—a bit on the strong side—and a wide pink-lipped mouth. If one studied those features objectively and separately, as he had done for innumerable hours, there was nothing outstanding about any of them.

And yet all together, she had the most beautiful face he had ever seen. It was full of character, full of laughter and full of love.

Or being a naive, arrogant young fool, so he had thought. Until his love for her had destroyed him, shattered him to pathetic pieces.

Leaning over the side of the lounger he was sitting on, Azeez extended his right hand. The movement pressed his hip into the chair and a sharp lance of pain shot up through it. Reaching the bottle of scotch, he took a quick sip.

The fiery liquid burned his throat and chest, making his vision another notch blurrier.

But the image in front of his eyes didn't waver. In fact, it became much more focused, as if it had been amplified and brought much closer for his very pleasure.

Because now he could see her long neck, the neck he had caressed with his fingers so long ago. The cheap, well-worn cotton draped loosely over her breasts, losing the fight to cover up their lushness. The fabric dipped neatly at the curve of her hip.

Wiping the back of his mouth with his hand, he grabbed the bottle with his other hand and stood up abruptly.

White-hot pain exploded in his right side, radiating from his hip, traveling up and down. He had been sitting for way too long today and had barely exercised since his brother had locked him up here in the palace.

Gritting his teeth, he breathed through the throbbing pain. He leaned against the pillar and looked up.

The sight that met his eyes stole his breath. The intense throbbing in his hip was nothing compared to the dark chasm opening up in his gut.

Because, now the mirage was torturing him.

The woman had tears in those beautiful eyes. Her lips whispered his name. Again and again, as though she couldn't help it, as though her very breath depended on saying his name.

In the mirage, the woman he had once loved more than anything else in life, the woman who had eventually destroyed him, was standing within touching distance. And for a man who had almost died happily, only to discover that he was alive, and a cripple at that, it was still the cruelest punishment to see her standing there, teasing him, tormenting him.

With a cry that never left his throat, he threw the bottle at the mirage, needing it to dissolve, needing the torturous cycle of self-loathing to abate.

Except, unlike all the other times he had done it, the woman flinched. Even as the bottle missed her, shattering as it hit the floor with a sound that fractured the silence.

Her soft gasp hit him hard in the gut, slicing through the drunken haze in his head. Shock waves pulsing through him, he moved as fast as his damaged hip would allow.

His fingers trembled as he extended his hand and touched her cheek. Her skin was as silky soft as he remembered. Bile filled his mouth and he had to suck in a harsh breath to keep it at bay. "Nikhat?"

Fear and self-loathing tangled inside him, his heart slamming hard against his rib cage.

The sheen of liquid in her beautiful dark brown eyes was real. The tremble in those rose-hued lips was real.

Azeez cursed, every muscle in his body freezing into ice. And before he could blink again, she was touching him, devouring him with her steady copper gaze.

She caught his roughened palm between hers, sending a jolt of sensation rioting through his body. It was as though a haze was lifted from his every sense, as though every nerve ending in him had been electrocuted into alertness. "Hello, Azeez."

He pushed her away from him and jerked back. Leaning against the pillar, he caught his breath, kept his eyes closed, waiting for the dancing spots in front of him to abate. He heard her soft exhale, heard the step she took toward him.

Suddenly, utter fury washed through him, ferociously hot in contrast to the cold that had frozen his very blood just a few minutes ago. "Who dared to let you in here? I might be a cripple but I'm still Prince Azeez bin Rashid Al Sharif of Dahaar. Get out before I throw you out myself."

Nikhat flinched, the walls she had built around herself denting at his words. But she couldn't let the bitterness of them seep in and become a part of her. This was not about her. "I have every right to be here, not that I think you're lucid enough to understand that."

He didn't snarl back at her as she expected.

He just stood there, staring at her, and she stared back, eight years of hunger ripping through all her stupid defenses.

Jet-black eyes set deep in his face, and even more now with the dark shadows beneath, gazed at her, a maelstrom of emotions blazing within. His aristocratic nose had a bump to it that hadn't been there before. It looked as if it had been broken and had never healed right.

And then came the most sensuous, cruelest mouth she had ever seen. Even before the terrorist attack, even before she had left him without looking back, he had had a fierce, dark smile that stole into her very skin and lodged there.

Being at the receiving end of that smile had been like being in the desert at night. When the Prince of Dahaar had looked at you, he demanded every inch of your focus and you gave it to him, willingly.

Right now, the same mouth was flattened into a rigid line.

The white, long-sleeved shirt he wore was open half-way through, showing his thin frame. His long hair curled over his collar.

"Leave, Nikhat. Now," he said, drawing her attention back to him. His gaze didn't linger on her face. He didn't meet her eyes, either. "Or I won't be responsible for what I do next."

"Apologize to me. That bottle could have done serious damage," she said, giving up the fight against herself.

The moment she had stepped out of her suite into the dimly lighted corridor, unable to sleep a wink, and wandered through this wing of the palace, wondering if he was nearby, exposing herself to the guard outside, she had given up any sense she'd ever had.

Only, she had thought she would take a quick look and slink away in the dark of the night. Self-delusion had never been her weakness and she couldn't let it take root now.

"No," Azeez said without compunction. "Didn't my brother warn you? You took the risk of visiting a savage animal in the middle of the night."

"I'm not afraid of you, Azeez. I never will be."

She took another step, bracing herself for the changes

in him. He had lost weight and it showed in his face. The sharp bridge of his nose, and those hollowed-out cheekbones, they stood out, giving him a gaunt, hard look.

"Ayaan told me about you last night," she said, opting for truth. One gut-wrenching lie was enough for this lifetime. "I couldn't wait. I...couldn't wait till morning."

He fisted his hands at his sides, his fury stamped into his features. "And?" he said in a low growl that gave her instant goose bumps. He clasped her cheek with his fingers, moving fast for a man in obvious pain. His grip was infuriatingly gentle yet she knew he was holding back a storm of fury.

His gaze collided with hers and what she saw there twisted her stomach; it was the one thing that did scare her. His eyes were empty, as though the spark that had been him, the very force of life that he had been, had died out.

"Have you seen enough, *latifa?* Is your curiosity satisfied?"

She clutched his wrists with her fingers, refusing to let him push her away.

And it wasn't for him. It was for her.

She hadn't cried when she had learned the news of the terrorist attack and of his death. Her heart had solidified into hard rock long before then. And she wouldn't cry now. But she allowed herself to touch him. She needed to know he was standing there. She touched his face, his shoulders, his chest, ignoring his sucked-in breath. "I'm so sorry. About Amira, about Ayaan, about you."

With a gentle grip, he pushed her back. There was nothing in his gaze when he looked at her. Not fury, not contempt, not even resentment. His initial shock had faded fast and he looked as if nothing she said would ever touch him. "Are you, truly?" he whispered.

"Yes."

"Why, Nikhat?"

She wasn't responsible for the terrorist attack, she knew that. And yet, nothing she had said to herself had prepared her for the tumult of seeing him like this.

"You're not responsible for what I've become. But if you want, you can do me a favor."

The force of his request didn't scare her. If she could do something to help him, she would. Ayaan had been right. She owed it to Azeez. "Anything, Azeez."

"Leave Dahaar before the sun is up. Leave and never come back. If you have ever felt anything true for me, Nikhat, do not show me your face ever again."

Nikhat stood rooted to the spot as he walked away from her. It seemed she was always going to disappoint him.

She couldn't leave now, just as she hadn't been able to stay when he had asked her eight years ago.

CHAPTER TWO

AYAAN PUT HIS coffee cup down on the breakfast table when he heard the sound that hammered at him with relentless guilt. The sound of his brother's approach.

Catching his wife's gaze, he saw the same shock coursing through him reflected in her eyes.

In the four months since he had practically dragged his brother to the palace, Azeez hadn't stepped foot into the breakfast hall once. Despite Ayaan's innumerable pleas. And today...

Ayaan signaled for the waiting staff to leave just as the sound of Azeez's harsh breathing neared the vast table. He pushed his chair back and looked up. Suddenly, the morning seemed brighter. "Would you like some cof—"

He never saw the punch coming. Shooting pain danced up and down his jaw as it landed, his vision blanking out for a few seconds.

Her loud, abrasive curse word ringing around them, his wife reached him instantly. Ayaan rubbed his jaw and looked up just in time to see Zohra march around his chair and push his brother in the chest.

Azeez's mouth was curved into a fiendish smile, and Ayaan was about to interfere, when Azeez stepped back from Zohra. He mocked a curtsy, his mouth curled into a sneer. "Good morning, Your Highness, you look...lovely."

"You are acting like an uncivilized thug," Zohra said, her gaze furious.

"*I am* an uncivilized thug, Princess Zohra," his brother replied with a hollow laugh. "And it is your husband who is keeping me here."

Flexing his jaw, Ayaan turned to his brother and froze.

Ferocious anger blazed out of that jet-black gaze he knew so well. The same gaze that had been filled with emptiness, indifference, for four months. The constant, hard knot in his gut relented just a little. "What was that for?"

"You are the future king of Dahaar, Ayaan, not of me. Keep your arrogant head out of my affairs."

Settling back down into his chair, Ayaan took a sip of his coffee. "I have no idea what you refer to, Azeez."

"I want her out of here."

The vehemence in his brother's words doubled his doubts. "Why are you so concerned about Nikhat's presence?"

Leaning his hip on the solid wood, Azeez bent. "I think all this power is going to your head. Don't manipulate me, little brother. Or I will—"

"What, Azeez?" Ayaan refused to back down. His cup clanged on the saucer in the ensuing silence, hot liquid spilling onto his fingers.

"You'll shoot yourself? I fell for that until now, but not anymore. If you were going to kill yourself, you had numerous chances to do it over the past six years. You would have been killed by that bullet. And yet here you are, stubborn as ever and intent on destroying yourself the hard way." Silence snarled between them. "Nikhat is not going anywhere. Not for at least six more months."

Emotion flashed in his brother's gaze but Ayaan had no idea which one.

"If your plan is to bring back memories that will suddenly fill me with a love for life, how about some good ones, Ayaan? Why don't you invite one of the numerous women I slept with six years ago to the palace?" He slanted a wicked glance at Zohra before looking at Ayaan again. "There used to be a particularly sexy stripper in that nightclub in Monaco who could do the wildest things with her tongue. If you want to see me rejoin the living, send the starchy doctor away, build a pole in my wing and have that stripper on a..."

His words tapering off, his brother looked as if he was the one dealt a punch.

Nikhat stood at the entrance to the hall. Against the colorful, blood-red rug on the wall behind her, she looked deathly pale. Their gazes locked on each other, Azeez and Nikhat stood unmoving, as if they were bound to each other.

Tension coiled tighter and tighter in the air around them.

His brother recovered first. And watching him closely, seeing a dark light come to life in his eyes, Ayaan realized that he'd made a terrible mistake.

"I'm regaling my brother and his wife with stories about Monaco. Was it the year right after you left?"

Beneath the humor, something else reverberated in Azeez's words, filling the vast hall with it.

"Does it matter *when* it was that you went around seducing the entire female population in Monaco, shaming Dahaar and your father with your wild exploits?" Nikhat delivered with equally lethal smoothness, even as her skin failed to recover its color.

Walking around Ayaan to Zohra's side, Nikhat whispered something to her. And walked out of the hall without another glance at his brother.

"Enough games, Ayaan. Why is she here?" Azeez roared the moment she left.

"Zohra is pregnant and is having complications. Nikhat is one of the best obstetricians in the country today. I need her to take care of my wife."

Azeez turned toward Zohra, his gaze assessing. "Congratulations to both of you. If she has to be here, keep her out of my way. Tell her she's forbidden from seeing me."

"I won't tell her any such thing. Nikhat is practically a member of this family. And she's doing me a favor. So unless you want to be my personal prisoner for the rest of your life, you better behave yourself."

"You've become a damn bastard, brother."

Ayaan laughed, the first in a long time he had truly done that. "I had to become one for Dahaar, Azeez. See, I wasn't born one like you are. It's the reason why you were so good at being the Crown Prince too. The minute you want it back, the crown's yours."

"That was a lifetime ago." Tight lines fanning around his mouth, Azeez stepped back. As if Ayaan had asked him to jump into the fiery pit of hell. "It's all yours now."

Azeez left the room, leaving a dark silence in his wake.

Once, his brother would have given his life to Dahaar. Once, a fire had shone in his eyes at the mere mention of it.

"Something's changed in him," Zohra said, a hint of warning in her voice. "And…Nikhat looked like she would break apart with one word from him."

Reaching for her outstretched hand on the table, Ayaan nodded. In four months of banging his head against the intractable wall that his brother had become, this was the first time there was a faint crack. He felt tremulous hope and excruciating guilt.

"Did you know if they were more than friends?"

Ayaan shook his head. He hadn't known before, but something his servant Khaleef had said in a throwaway comment had stuck with him. So he had taken a gamble and commanded Nikhat's father to summon her.

Being right had never left such an ugly taste in his mouth.

After a couple of wrong turns, Nikhat reached the court-yard behind the wing she had been shown to three days ago. High walls surrounded the courtyard, shielding it from any curious gazes.

It was only ten in the morning but the sun was already bright and hot. Wiping the beads of sweat on her forehead, she sat down on the bench near a magnificent fountain. The rhythmic swish of the water, the scent of roses coating the air…it was a feast for the senses, but she couldn't get her stretched nerves to relax.

For three days, she had been busy with Princess Zohra and yet going out of her mind, intensely curious to see Azeez again.

She had dreamed of him so many times when she had thought him dead, had imagined all the things she would say if she had one more chance to see him, to touch him, to hold him…

Reality, however, didn't afford her the same reckless-ness.

Closing her eyes, she leaned back and felt the sun caress her face. She couldn't let him unsettle her any more than she could weave silly dreams again just because he was back from the dead.

She would be of no use to Ayaan either way.

Taking her Crocs off, she dipped her toes in the water. It was forbidden to do so, but the cold water tickled her feet. Drops splashed onto her leggings. Her jet lag was gone, but she still wasn't used to the quiet that surrounded her after the mad rush back in the hospital in New York. Nor was she happy with the way things were run here, even though she had known to expect it.

Even with Ayaan's command that she was solely in charge of Zohra's care, her instructions had been met with resistance from the numerous medical advisers and staff that surrounded the Princess. Which only made her realize how much she would need the royal family's backing to succeed in Dahaar and even more resolute to make a difference.

It couldn't have been more than two minutes when her skin prickled in alarm. The hairs on the back of her neck stood up. The relentless heat of the day receded for a minute. A shadow. Her heart stuttering in her chest, she realized who stood over here, stealing the warmth from around her.

Keeping her eyes closed, she took a moment to pull herself together. She opened her eyes slowly and sat up straighter on the bench.

His gait uneven, Azeez walked to the bench on her left. His face tightened, his right hand flexing into a fist as he slowly slid into the seat.

He hadn't shaved and the beard coming in made him look even more dangerous. His eyes still had that haggard, bruised look, the planes of his cheekbones prominent.

The pristine white shirt hung loose on his frame while his cotton trousers hung low and loose on his hips. They made him look darker than usual, but not enough to hide the tiredness from his face.

His will was a force of nature and offense was her best course if she wanted to get through. She made no effort to curb the stinging comment that rose to her lips. "That hip will be permanently useless if you continue like this. Even in the state you're in, I believe…"

Those thickly lashed eyes trapped hers, a puzzle in it. She couldn't have looked away for anything in the world.

Everything else she could control, curb, but not the greedi-ness with which she wanted to look at him. "I believe you still have enough sense to know that."

"*Ya Allah*, stop looking at me like that." His low growl rumbled over the silent courtyard.

"How am I looking at you?" she said, tucking her feet beneath her legs.

He leaned his head back, giving her a perfect view of the strong column of his neck. Even dressed in the most casual clothes, he epitomized supreme male arrogance and confidence that had always messed with her usually prac-tical personality. And continued to do so, if she was ready to admit the truth. "Like you cannot stop, like you want to eat me up alive."

The heat rising through her cheeks had nothing to do with the sun. "That's not true."

He leaned forward, his gaze thoughtful. "Yes, it is. There's a temerity in your gaze now. You always knew your own mind, but now, it's like your body has caught up."

She shrugged, holding herself tight and still under his scrutiny. The look he cast in her direction was thorough. "I'm not a shy twenty-two-year-old anymore."

"I can see that." A lick of something came alive in his gaze. "I can almost see you staring down your patients into good health."

She laughed, half to hide the little tremble that went through her. "I do have a reputation as the scary doctor. If only things could be fixed so simply. And you're right. I can't stop looking at you. I can't stop wondering what in Allah's name you think you're doing to yourself."

His jaw tightened, his nostrils flared.

For anyone looking from afar, they would seem like two old friends chatting up each other. And yet the court-yard felt like a minefield. She had to take every step carefully with him. And not because she was scared of him, but of herself.

Her stupid midnight jaunt had already proved her brain wasn't functioning at its normal, rational level.

He ran his palm over his jaw, his gaze never moving from her. "Is it true?"

"Is what true?"

"The palace has been ringing with it. And apparently, it is the first time in three days that you have a minute to yourself."

"So you're not completely oblivious to the world around you? That's always a good sign."

"Don't show off your credentials with me, Nikhat. Is Princess Zohra having complications with the pregnancy?"

There was no nuance to his words. She had no idea if he was worried for the Princess, no way to gauge how deep the emptiness in him was. And more than anything, the very thought she might not be of any use to him scared her. "Yes."

"How serious is it?"

"I have ordered some more tests for her. Her blood pressure is at dangerous levels. She needs rest and she needs to take it easy. Stress is adding to her complications. From what I've seen in the last two days, you're at the root of it."

"Just because I punched her husband?"

"You punched Ayaan? Why?"

Because Ayaan had brought her here, the answer came to her in the taut silence.

Do you hate me so much?

The pathetic, self-indulgent question lingered on her lips. But there was no point in asking it. There was no point in giving the past even a passing thought.

"You have really changed," she said, hoping to find a hole in that indifference he wore like armor, hoping to land a blow. "The Azeez I knew would have never lifted his hand against his brother, would have never thrown a bottle at an innocent, harmless woman."

He chuckled, and the unexpected sound of it shocked her. Sharp grooves appeared in his cheeks. "You are neither innocent nor harmless. I was drunk. It was your own fault for walking into a man's wing in the middle of the night where you're forbidden."

"And you throw bottles at imaginary figures when you are drunk?"

"Only at you."

The barb cut through her, knocking her air from her lungs. She drew in a jagged breath, swiping her gaze away from him. This was the future she had wanted to avoid eight years ago—his resentment, his bitterness. Because Azeez had never hidden from what he felt, neither had he let her. And yet, after everything she had done, she was right where she didn't want to be—the cause of that resentment.

She looked up and found him studying her with a curious intensity. "I'm serious, Azeez. Princess Zohra needs to rest and relax. Unless you do something that allays her concerns for Ayaan, she's only going to get worse.

"She...loves Ayaan very much. And the fact that he's worried about you is directly transferring to her."

"She's the future of Dahaar. I don't want anything to happen to her."

Did he realize he had betrayed himself? From everything Ayaan had said, Azeez had claimed he didn't care about anything. "Is it only the future of Dahaar that concerns you? Not what you are doing to Ayaan, to your parents? To yourself?"

He shot to his feet so quickly that Nikhat jerked her head up. Just in to time to see the flash of pain in his face. "This is where this session ends. You're not my friend. You're definitely not my doctor.

"You're a servant to the royal family. Do your job. Look after Princess Zohra. Believe me, there's nothing you can do to help me. Except disappear, maybe."

"I'm not leaving, Azeez. Not until I accomplish my job. And as to Ayaan's belief in me, I've never let down the royal family's trust in me until now and I never will."

"Never, Nikhat?"

Her breath trapped in her throat, Nikhat hugged herself. "Never."

Nodding, he came to a stop at the wide arched entrance, the sun shining behind him casting shadows on his features. She had no idea what he saw in the mirror when he looked at himself, what tormented him from the past. But the fact that he was here, concerned for the Princess, gave her hope like nothing else could.

"I never thought of you as naive."

Uncoiling her legs from under her, she took a moment to compose herself. The last thing she wanted was him talking about her. "I used to be. But not anymore. I'm not the girl you once knew, Azeez."

"Why obstetrics of all the specializations? Why not cardiology?"

She stayed painfully still, amazed at how easily, even after all these years, he could drill down to the heart of the matter. How well he knew her.

"Your mother's been dead for eighteen years, Nikhat. You cannot save her or the child she died giving birth to."

It took everything in her for Nikhat to stay standing.

"Do I need to have your case history checked?"

"What do you mean?"

"Princess Zohra is valuable to Ayaan and Dahaar." This time, Dahaar was the afterthought to his brother. "Will you be able to keep your objectivity when the time comes? Or are you fighting a never-ending battle with yourself and trying to save your mother again and again?"

She flinched, his words finding their mark. She could feel the blood leaving her face, but in this, she would not keep quiet. In this, she would not let him find fault.

"Hate me all you want, Azeez, but don't you dare insult my ability as a doctor or my reasons for it. I chose obstetrics because, with all the progress your family has made for Dahaar, there are so many things in women's health that are still backward, so many antiquated notions that dictate a woman's life.

"My profession has nothing to do with the past. It's my life, my future."

"As long as you are remember that, Dr. Zakhari. Because you paid a high price for that, didn't you?"

Nikhat sank back to the seat, her own lie coming back to haunt her.

He still thought she had left him because her love for her dream had been more than her love for him. And crushed under the weight of the truth, she had let him believe the lie.

She *had* paid a high price. She had paid with her heart, with her love. She had paid for something she couldn't change. And she had meticulously built her life from all the broken pieces to let even the Prince of Dahaar shatter it.

CHAPTER THREE

AZEEZ LEANED AGAINST the wall outside Ayaan's office and sucked in a harsh breath. Sweat trickled down his shoulder blades after the long walk from his wing to this side of the palace. Closing his eyes, he rubbed his palm over the right hip, willing the shooting pain to relent.

But of course it didn't. He'd spent the past four months drinking himself into oblivion, uncaring of if he ate or moved. His negligence was coming back to him in the form of excruciating pain. His hip was sore from months of inactivity, from lack of exercise. Breathing in and out through the dots dancing in front of him, he slowly sank to the floor.

His brother had been right. There had been more than one occasion when he had wished himself dead. But he hadn't actually indulged the thought of killing himself.

His list of sins was already long enough without committing one against God, too. So he had carried on, uncaring of anything, uncaring of what a wasteland his life had become.

But his self-loathing, his lack of interest in his life, his lack of respect for his own body—as long as it had been only him who faced the consequences, he had been fine with it. But now...

Now it was beginning to fester into his brother and his wife.

After everything he had gone through, after recovering from the blood loss because of the bullet wound he had taken during the terrorist attack, waking up amidst strangers with a useless leg, realizing what he had become, after the excruciating pain of keeping himself away from his family, he could not allow this.

Whatever rot was in him couldn't be allowed to spread, couldn't be allowed to contaminate the good that was finally happening in his family. He couldn't be allowed to take more from them, from Dahaar.

And if the price was that he give up the last ounce of his self-respect, if the price was that he stop hiding and face his demons, face the reality of everything he had ruined with his reckless actions, then so be it. He couldn't have escaped the consequences of his actions forever anyway.

"Azeez?" Ayaan's question reached his ears, unspoken, guarded, with a wealth of pain in it.

Azeez licked his lips and cleared his throat. The words stuck to his tongue. He forced himself to speak them. "Help me up, Ayaan."

For a few seconds, his brother didn't move. His shock pinged against the corridor walls in the deafening silence. Gritting his teeth, Azeez strove to keep his bitterness out of his words. "Do you want to exact revenge for that punch I threw three days ago?" he mocked. "Will you help me if I beg, Your Highness?"

A curse flying from his mouth, Ayaan spurred into action. Shaking his head, he tucked his hands under Azeez's shoulders. "On three."

Azeez nodded, and took a deep breath. He gripped Ayaan's wrists and pulled himself up.

Ayaan leaned against the opposite wall and folded his arms. "Is it always like this?" There was anger in his brother's words and beneath it, a sliver of pain.

Curbing the stinging response that rose to his lips, Azeez shook his head. "It's my own fault. The less mobile I'm, the worse the hip gets."

"Why didn't you just summon me then?"

"I never did that. You are the one forever coming into my suite for one of your bonding sessions."

Frowning, Ayaan opened the door behind him and held it for Azeez. Azeez stepped inside and froze.

Smells and sensations, echoes of laughter and joy, they assaulted him from all sides, poking holes in his deceptively thin armor.

A chill broke out over his skin as his gaze fell on the majestic desk at the far corner. A wooden, handmade box that had been in the Al Sharif dynasty for more than two centuries. The gold-embossed fountain pen that had passed on through generations, from father to son, from king to king. And the sword on display in a glass case to the right.

The sword he had been presented in the ceremony when his father had announced him the Crown Prince and future King, the sword that had represented everything he had been. Now, it was his brother's, and Azeez didn't doubt for a minute that it was where it belonged.

A portrait of their family hung behind the leather chair.

The smiling face of his sister, Amira, punched him in the gut. He had killed her as simply as if he had done it with both his hands.

Enough.

He hadn't come here to revisit his mistakes. He'd come to stop more from happening.

Shying his gaze away from the portrait, he walked toward the sitting area on the right and slid into a chaise longue. Ayaan followed him and took the opposite seat.

"Nikhat says it's because of me," he said without preamble. He needed to say his piece and get out. He needed to be out of this room, needed to be back in the cavern of self-loathing that his suite had become. Before the very breath was stifled out of him by broken expectations, by excruciating guilt.

Ayaan frowned. "What is because of you?"

"Zohra's complications with the pregnancy."

His mouth tight, a mask fell over his brother's usually expressive face. Cursing himself for how self-absorbed he had been, Azeez studied him, noticing for the first time the stress on Ayaan's face.

Dark blue shadows hung under his brother's eyes. His skin was drawn tight over his gaunt features.

"I wouldn't put it quite like that," Ayaan spoke finally, with a sigh. "For reasons the doctors say they can't speculate over, it's been a high-risk pregnancy from the beginning."

"Then what did Nikhat mean by saying it was because of me? I know she didn't say that to manipulate me."

"I thought you didn't want to see her or hear a word from her mouth. Now you trust her opinion?"

"Nikhat wanted to be a doctor since she was ten years old. If there's one thing that she would never betray, it's her profession. So if she says I'm the reason for Zohra's stress, then I am. What I don't understand is why. I might be a cripple but I have a working mind."

"Do you? Because, so far, I haven't seen evidence of it."

Azeez continued as though his usually even-tempered brother hadn't just snarled at him. "I have watched your wife growl at me like a lioness, as if she needs to shield you from me. I don't think she would crumble because her husband is dealing with his difficult brother. So what is it, Ayaan?"

A flash of utter desolation came alive in his brother's gaze. Azeez stared, shock waves shivering through him.

Ever since he had learned that Ayaan had returned after six years, Azeez had known that his brother would do his duty, no matter what. And Ayaan *had* risen to every challenge.

Only now did Azeez realize what he had overlooked. His brother had fought his own demons for so long and Azeez had not given a passing thought to it until this moment.

"She's worried about what this—" he moved his hand between Azeez and him "—is doing to me."

A chilly finger raked its nail over Azeez's spine. "What do you mean?"

"I have nightmares, vicious ones. I have had them every night ever since I… since I became lucid. Sometimes, they are minimal. Sometimes, I get violent. And…"

Azeez held his head in his hands, feeling his breath leave him. Guilt infused his blood, turning him cold from inside out. Looking up, he forced himself to speak the words. "They have become worse since you found me."

Ayaan shrugged.

There was no shame or hesitation in his brother's gaze. Only resigned acceptance. And in that minute, Azeez realized what he had been too blind to see until now.

His brother had lived through his own version of hell and had come out of it alive and honorable. And Dahaar was blessed to have him.

Unless he, Azeez, ruined it all again.

"I keep reliving that night and every time I see all that blood in the stable, your blood, I wake up screaming. And Zohra is right there with me, suffering through them, right by me."

"Why didn't you tell me?"

"When would I have told you? In between the punches you threw at Khaleef and me? When you refused point-blank to see Mother even though you could hear her heart-breaking cries on the other side of the door and informed

Father to assume that his firstborn is still dead? Or in the few hours that you have been sober in the last four months?"

Azeez shifted in the seat restlessly. He wanted to run away from here. "Be rid of me," he growled, his powerlessness eating through his insides. "All this will be solved in a minute."

Ayaan rocked forward onto his knees, a fierce scowl on his face. "You think I can just wish away your existence as you have been doing?"

"Then send your wife away. Protect her."

"I can't," Ayaan said, a sarcastic chuckle accompanying his words. "I am to be crowned king in two months, but I can't dictate my wife's behavior. I have ordered her to sleep in a separate wing, to go back to Siyaad for a few days. But, like you cleverly noticed, my wife has a will of her own. She won't leave my side."

From the moment he had met her steady gaze, Azeez had realized how much Princess Zohra loved his brother. Something he had wanted once, something he had thought he had once.

He swallowed back the surge of envy that gripped him. He would not envy the little happiness that Ayaan had. This had to stop today, now. "Fine. What is it you want from me?"

"What?"

"Tell me what you want me to do. Tell me what I can do to make this…make you better and take this stress off Zohra."

"Why now, when you have all but thrown back my requests in my face?"

"Because there's already too much blood on my hands and I don't want more."

Ayaan's face tightened, his gaze filled with pity that Azeez didn't want. "Azeez, that's not—"

"This is your chance to protect your wife, Ayaan. Don't waste it on useless matters."

"Fine," his brother said, standing up. "I want you to take care of yourself. I want you to have physiotherapy, I want you to see a psychiatrist, and I want you to see Mother and I want you at my coronation in a—"

"Don't push it," Azeez said, feeling the shackles of his brother's demands binding him to Dahaar. Just the word *coronation* was like sticking a steel spike into his heart.

With his hand on the armrest, he pushed himself off the chaise. There was only one choice left to him, only one solution to stop the ruin he had begun again. And everything within him revolted at it. "I will do this, but I will do it my own way."

"What do you mean?"

"I won't see a team of doctors. Nikhat can attend to me in between attending to Zohra."

"Azeez," his brother's voice rang with warning as Azeez walked toward the exit, keeping his gaze away from everything in the room. "Whatever you are planning to do, don't. She is here by my request."

"Exactly. *You* brought her into this, Ayaan. Now that I'm following your orders, don't complain about it."

Stepping outside his brother's office, Azeez slowly made his way back to his own quarters. He still planned to leave Dahaar. For his own sanity, he had to.

But he would postpone it until things were right with Princess Zohra. And he couldn't live the rest of his life the way he had been doing, either.

He would do what his brother asked him to do because nothing else would be enough for Ayaan. However, there was no point in a team of doctors poking through his head. There was nothing anyone could do to fix him.

But Dr. Zakhari, he had been mistaken to dismiss her

so quickly. She owed him. And she would become his route to freedom from this palace, from a life that would slowly but surely do what a bullet hadn't been able to do— kill him.

Nikhat finished her dinner and dismissed the maid from her quarters. Ten seconds later, she couldn't remember what it was that had been served to her in the glittering silverware.

She only remembered looking at her reflection in the plate, rushing to the long, oval mirror in her bedroom and redoing her unruly hair.

She stood before it again now, going over herself with a critical eye. Her long-sleeved, high-collared caftan in unrelenting black was made of a stiff silk that instead of clinging to her breasts sat on her shoulders like a tent. Small diamond studs, a gift she had given herself for her thirtieth birthday, were her only jewelry.

Sighing loudly, she grabbed another pin and slapped it over one strand of hair that refused to sit back in her braid. Satisfied with how she looked, she pressed her temples with her fingers and massaged.

She was used to braiding her hair back tight for the operating room. But this time, she had done it so tight that her head ached.

She checked the pile of gifts she had spent hours wrapping, unable to sit still. Had she known that Princess Zohra would allow her father to come straight into Nikhat's suite in the far-off wing of the palace that housed her, she would have straightened a little more. As it was, she had made the maid nervous with her own twitching and needed to dismiss her.

Pulling her sleeve back, she checked her watch again. Her father was due any minute.

She was pacing the floor, wearing out the ancient, priceless rug when a knock sounded. Her feet flying on the floor, she opened the door.

And froze.

Azeez stood on the other side of the threshold. His jaw was clean-shaven, his gaze steady, a glimpse of the old him peeking out of it. She had forgotten the compelling effect his very presence held.

Her already strung-out nerves stretched a little more.

The fact that he was a few doors away in the same wing as her, night and day, rang like an unrelenting bell in the back of her head however busy she was. Seeing him outside her suite, in the palace of all the places, was a shock that needed its own category.

"I need to speak with you."

He didn't wait for her answer. In true arrogant-prince fashion, he pushed his way past her into the suite. Flustered at his sudden appearance, Nikhat turned around.

"Close your mouth, Nikhat. And the door."

She shut her mouth, not the door. Hopefully she looked defiant, because inside she was trembling. "Why?"

The curve of his mouth turned up in a smirk, his gaze shining with an unholy light. That spark, that smile, had once played havoc with her senses, and apparently it still could. Because her legs were barely holding her up.

"Are you afraid to be alone with me?"

She closed the door shut behind her with a thud that should have silenced the resounding yes in her head.

Her luxurious and vast suite, which had mocked all her New York sophistication, suddenly seemed impossibly small with him standing in the middle of it. He was like the sun, reducing everything around him to colorless insignificance.

Standing close, his gaze moved over her like a caress.

"Why are you dressed in that awful thing? And what happened to your hair?"

Nikhat stared back at him, all her worldliness, her sophistication, sliding away like sand between her fingers.

She had prepared herself to bear the brunt of his contempt, even hatred, in the coming months. But his attention, especially of a personal nature? No amount of preparation could help her deal with it.

"If this is how you dress usually, no wonder they were so happy to be rid of you in New York."

"I left of my own volition. I left a good position in a cutting-edge hospital to come back." Too late, she realized he was playing with her. His whole demeanor today was different. It was as if he had a strategy, as if all the fire of his emotions was neatly packed away for now. And even as he cut through her with his acerbic words, she still preferred him like that. The real him. "To build something that's very much needed here in Dahaara."

"Ah....I heard about all your plans for the clinic. Princess's Zohra's pregnancy, Ayaan's desperation to fix me, your history with me, everything's falling into place for you, isn't it? Like always."

Anger burst through her. "You think it's easy for to me to be back here? To leave behind the freedom, the position, the respect I had in New York? To constantly fight against invisible prejudices just because I'm a woman? Even being the Princess's personal physician is still apparently not recommendation enough."

"If you expected anything different, then you're a fool, Nikhat."

"Because I want to change some things for the better in Dahaar? You had a dream like that once, Azeez. Or have you completely wiped out everything from the past?"

He remained unflappable, even as her temper soared.

"You chose a difficult path for yourself and an even harder one by coming back. Why stay if it's so hard?"

"Because I know that I can make a difference. I want all the hard work I put in to amount to something for Dahaar. And I refuse to let any prejudice masquerading as tradition stop me."

His silence this time didn't grate on her. Because being back in Dahaar was harder not only on a professional level but a personal one. She had tasted freedom in New York. She could go wherever she wanted, she could talk to whomever she wanted to, without written permission, without seeing questions lingering in gazes wherever she turned.

"No, you never stray from your path once you decide, do you?" A grudging respect filled his words. "Just don't expect any changes overnight, Nikhat."

She nodded, fiercely glad for this discussion. Because even if he said his words in a mocking tone, Azeez gave her a sense of being understood that she needed so much.

"So, dressing like you're going to your own execution is the first step to convince everyone here to take you seriously?"

She raised a brow and smiled, smoothing a hand over the stiff silk. "Your mask of indifference in slipping, Azeez. You sound rather interested in how I'm dressed."

Something playful entered his gaze as he shrugged. "You look like a black hole, Nikhat. Unless you tell me why, I will assume it's to dissuade my interest. Then I'll have to inform you that I would rather take another bullet in the hip than touch you."

Heat flaring under her skin, Nikhat glared at him. "My father is coming to see me any minute. And my sisters. If you need me to be your punching bag, I would like to schedule the session for some other time that suits me better."

She checked her watch again, unable to contain her anxiety.

"You have to look like this to see your father? Is this some new law that Ayaan passed?"

She looked down at herself, knowing he was right. But she didn't want to give her father any more reason to be angry with her, or to find fault with her in any way. Loneliness she had battled for eight years solidified in her throat. "I…I have not seen him in eight years, Azeez. My sisters… can you imagine what Noor would look like now?" she said, thinking of her youngest sister. "Please, just leave, for now. I don't have the luxury to turn my back on my family like you have done."

The humor faded from his face. "Why didn't you see them all these years?"

"My father's condition for when I left Dahaar to study was that I not return. What you don't know, and I didn't realize, is how intractable he is. He forbade me from seeing him or my sisters."

Before he could reply, a knock sounded on the door. Panic tying her stomach in knots, she grasped his hands and jerked back as the contact sent a jolt of sensation through her. "Please, Azeez," she whispered, turning toward the door.

With a hard look at her, he walked around the sitting area and into her bedroom.

Only after she heard the click behind her did Nikhat's heart settle back into place. Wiping her forehead with the back of her hand, she opened the wide, double doors.

The smile froze on her mouth when she saw her father, alone. "Hello, Father," she said, unable to pull her gaze away from the eerily silent corridor.

His hands folded behind him, her father stepped into the suite. He stood there stiffly, casting a glance around the room, not a hint of warmth in his gaze or welcome in his stance.

Swallowing back her disappointment, Nikhat gestured toward the seating area. "Would you like something to drink?"

"I cannot stay long, Nikhat. There's an urgent security issue that I have to address with Prince Ayaan."

Nikhat nodded. "I understand how busy you are. I just... I thought the girls were coming with you."

His gaze remained steady on her, nothing betrayed in his set face. "I wished to make sure it was suitable for them to visit you here."

"It's the palace, Father. It's the most secure place in Dahaar. Ayaan said—" She caught herself at the spark of displeasure in his tight mouth. "Prince Ayaan informed me himself that I have permission to have guests. I'm the personal physician to the Crown Princess, not a prisoner of state," she said, bitterness spewing into her words.

"I did not think you were a prisoner." Even more hardness settled into his features, making his expression intractable. "I have heard rumors, however. Nothing I would repeat. In fact, it is what I need to address with the Crown Prince. But between the rumors and his sudden command to call you back to Dahaar, I do not like the conclusions I had to draw."

Anger filled her, replacing the powerlessness that had been clawing at her. All she wanted was to see her sisters. One small thing. And it seemed as if the whole universe was conspiring to deny her that. "What are these conclusions, Father?"

"I will not repeat them. And certainly not in front of you."

Hot fury filled every inch of her. "Yes, you will. I am your daughter and I'm thirty years old. I have lived outside

Dahaar, in a foreign land among strangers for eight years. Without any man's protection, I have seen the world. I have not only taken care of myself but I have also flourished in my career. If I'm being denied the chance to see my own sisters—" she knew she was shouting at him now, that her voice was breaking, but she didn't care anymore "—you will damn well tell me why not."

"Swearing when you speak to your father? Is this what you have become?"

She gritted her teeth. For so many years, she had kept quiet. Even before she left Dahaar, she had always tried to be a model daughter, tried to be the son he had always wanted. "What have I become? What have I done that is so wrong that you're still punishing me for it?"

He shook his head and Nikhat felt the one thing she had wanted slipping away from her hands. Everything she had achieved amounted to nothing if she still couldn't see her sisters. "You owe me the truth at least."

"Who are you serving, Nikhat? The Crown Princess Zohra or Prince Azeez?"

Nikhat could feel the blood fading from her face. "You cannot mention your suspicions to anyone. You cannot betray them."

Her father flinched. "I would never betray the royal family. It's all the small things I've been hearing. And no one else can come to the conclusion as I have. You and Prince Azeez…" He looked away from her as though his very thoughts were shameful. "I knew there was something between you all those years ago. Time and again I reminded you to keep your distance from them, to remember the disparity between our life and theirs. You never paid any attention to my warnings. You never do once you settle on something."

Nikhat tried to wrap her mind around what he was saying. The truth of it shone in his unforgiving eyes.

He had known she had been in love with Azeez and he had assumed she had left Dahaar because her relationship with the prince had fallen apart. She didn't know whether to laugh or cry at how perceptive her father was. "I have never done anything to bring shame upon you." Even when she had known that she had to walk away, she had still refused herself what she wanted more than anything in the world.

"It does not matter. But if the Crown Prince has summoned you back to the palace, if he's keeping you here because he thinks it will...*help* Prince Azeez...then I can't risk bringing your sisters here. Your life, your reputation, it's out of my hands. You took the right to protect you away from me when you left Dahaar. When you finish this...assignment, you will leave again. Leave whatever scandal you might create behind you. Your sisters have to live here, marry and make their lives. And I am still their father. I have to protect them."

"What would you have me do, Father? Deny the Crown Prince's request after everything King Malik has done for this family?"

"No, do your duty, whatever it...entails." Tight lines fanned his mouth, and Nikhat knew what it cost him to say those words. And yet, it didn't shock or surprise her. Her father had served King Malik for forty years. His loyalty was what had brought Nikhat to the palace to be educated at Princess Amira's side. "But do not ask me to involve your sisters in this. Not until whatever you are doing for the Crown Prince is finished, not until I know this will not affect their reputation."

Without another word, he walked out, shattering her hopes.

Nikhat slid to the seat behind her, too shaken to even shed tears.

She had thought that she had molded life to suit her will, that she had survived through her biggest pain, that she could tackle anything life threw at her, and yet, back in Dahaar, when it came to the one thing that truly mattered to her, she was truly powerless.

Useless rage boiled over inside her, the urge to pack up and leave without looking back pounding through her blood.

She heard Azeez's slow gait coming toward her. And for once, she couldn't care to hide her desolation.

He came to a standstill on her right, leaning against the dark chaise her father had just vacated. "And here I thought Ayaan had convinced you to whore yourself out to me in return for your big clinic? A reunion with your family is the prize you're going for?"

Anger burst through her, liberating and consuming, fraying the last rope of hope that had been holding her together. His words cheapened everything they had once shared, minimized everything she had become.

She shot to her feet, and reached him, adrenaline pumping through her blood. The force of her fury shaking through her, she slapped him hard.

The sharp sound reverberated around them, the impact of it jarring her arm, shaking her very breath.

He ran a hand over his jaw, an unholy light shining in his eyes. "Feel better?"

Her stomach folding on itself, she fisted her hand to stop the tremors. He hadn't even tried to stop her.

She had played directly into his hands. His gaze burned with a fire that she knew not to go near. But she couldn't step back, couldn't break eye contact with him. "You provoked me on purpose."

Pity and something indefinable danced in his gaze. "You looked like you would perish from the grief running through you, like you would never hope again. It was either I slap you or you slap me."

She didn't want to owe him more than she already did. "Now you know what we all see when we look at you."

She thought he would laugh at her. Instead, a thoughtful look dawned on his face. "Is that why you are here, Nikhat? Because you pity me?"

Folding her arms, she faced him. "That's the one thing I can truthfully say I have never felt for you, Azeez. You make it hard to pity you."

Relief dawned in his gaze. With his hands gripping the armrest, he sank into the chaise. "Ayaan will order your father to let you see them. He will have no choice but to follow his orders. Having to choose between your family and your profession, or anything else, is not something anyone should have to face."

Their gazes held, a wealth of memories fighting for breath in the air around them. He had spoken those words to her before too. He had made promises and he had kept every single one of them.

She…she had made one promise. And she hadn't been able to keep it.

Shaking her head, she pushed those memories back to where they belonged. "My father's right. I don't know where I'm going to be in six months' time. With a future so uncertain, it is better I stay away from my sisters."

"Or you could simply leave. I will help you get out of the palace. Ayaan will not force you to return."

"Are you so eager to be rid of me, Azeez?" She regretted the words the instant they were out.

"Yes, I would like nothing more than for you to leave,"

he said with crippling honesty that had always been a part of him.

Taking the option he was giving her, going back to New York where she had unfettered freedom, where her every movement, small and big, wasn't dictated by someone else, away from the man looking up at her with a dark fire that drew her nearer every day, it was the easiest thing to do.

She could save both of them from the misery of reliving a painful past because, try as she might, it kept rearing up its head.

And she wouldn't feel this desolation at being so close to her sisters and still not seeing them. But the same loyalty that was in her father's blood filled hers too.

"I made a promise to Ayaan. Whatever happens in the next few months, I want to live in Dahaara. I want to head that clinic. There's a lot of good I can do here."

He rubbed his forehead with long fingers. "Of course. You have goals, and plans to accomplish those goals. And if something fails, you dust yourself off and move on."

"Why did you come here, Azeez?"

"I want you to help me convince Ayaan that everything is wonderfully perfect up here," he said, poking himself in the head.

"So that you can leave the palace and get yourself killed?"

"I don't have to leave the palace to accomplish that." He said the words softly, slowly, as if he was crushed by a weight he couldn't shake. He stood up from the chaise and walked toward the door, his frame tight with tension. When he met her gaze, the depth of pain in it shook her. And they all thought he didn't care, that he had become a shell of his former self. "I cannot bear to be here, Nikhat. I have to convince Ayaan that leaving Dahaar is the best thing for me, for him, for our parents. I have to leave Dahaar. And it has to be done in such a way that Ayaan feels no guilt."

Nikhat shook her head. "That's a tall order. I'll never be able to convince him, because I don't think it is the best thing for you."

"But you will do it."

The arrogance in his tone stole her breath away. "Why will I do it?"

He leaned against the wall, his hand gripping his hip. "Do you want me to die a slow, painful death?"

A shiver went through her at the desolation in his eyes. She reached him, desperate to relieve his pain, desperate to do something. "Azeez, you can't—"

He threw an arm out as if to halt her from coming near him. When he spoke, it was through gritted teeth. "This palace is eating me up alive. Everywhere I turn, I see the destruction I have wrought on Ayaan, on my parents, on Dahaar itself. If I have to live, it has to be outside these palace walls."

Dahaar had once been an integral part of him, his life, his blood, his passion. To hear him say it was stifling the life out of him was the most painful thing she had ever heard.

For whatever reason, Azeez held himself responsible for everything that happened, and as long as he did, he couldn't breathe in here. Broken dreams, and ghosts of a glorious past, the palace was full of it—it was a pain she felt, an agony that she understood.

Which meant she had no choice but to agree.

What he was asking of her, it was a betrayal of her promise to Ayaan, a betrayal of the promise she had made to herself. But, as it always had been, when it came to Azeez, nothing else mattered to her. Not even her own happiness.

She wanted him to live, and if she could help him do that the way he wanted, then so be it. "I will help you, Azeez," she heard herself say.

And was rewarded by a puzzled nod from him.

CHAPTER FOUR

NIKHAT FOLLOWED THE palace maid down a maze of intricate marble-lined corridors, her heart slowly climbing up her throat with every step she took.

Agreeing to Azeez's proposal was one thing. Venturing into his suite with an action plan in hand, another. At least, Ayaan had been pleasantly surprised when she had informed him what she had in mind, during Princess Zohra's morning checkup.

With a nod, the maid pointed her to intricately designed double doors and left. Clutching her iPad with shaking fingers, she stepped over the threshold and stilled at the utter magnificence of the suite. She had thought her suite was the lap of luxury. Compared to this one, hers was more like a storage room, in sheer size and the magnificence of it.

She had been here that first night, but in her anxiety to see Azeez, she had paid no attention to her surroundings. She had spent innumerable hours in the palace, roamed most of the corridors and wings with Amira, everywhere but here. Because it was the Prince's wing and had been forbidden to all of them.

Azeez's suite, she discovered, looking past the main area, backed onto private gardens and was a cavernous bedchamber rather than a mere suite. She walked past the vast foyer into the main area and stilled. Her breath hitched in her throat. Cream-colored walls flowed seamlessly against the similarly colored marble floors, inlaid here and there with gold piping. She knew it was gold because she had once asked Amira, her mouth falling open to her chest.

Dark red velvet curtains brocaded with gold threads hung heavily beside the floor-length windows. A sitting area was on her left containing gilt-edged sofas and chaise lounges with claw-feet made in intricate detail. Lush Persian rugs in colorful designs lay here and there. A silver tea service, along with a variety of mouthwatering dishes on the table, all lay untouched.

A crystal decanter, which looked as old and priceless as the rest of the trappings of the room, stood next to the tray, the gold liquid swirling at the bottom telling its own story.

Against the opposite wall sat a vast bed, almost waist high, with a wide, intricately designed metal headboard, and sheets again of the darkest red. A velvet-covered stool stood off to the side.

Cushions and pillows of every possible size lay haphazardly atop the sheets. A white cotton shirt was at the foot of the bed that looked half crumpled.

Her feet carried her to the bed—because really she had no idea she had decided to walk toward it. A hint of sandalwood, underlaid with a scent that was *his,* reached her nose, invading her skin with a lick of heat.

She sucked in greedy bursts, drawing it deep into her lungs before she realized that she was doing it. The sheets were soft and warm against her shaking fingers, and her mind conjured an image of him tangled in them.

A low, thrilling pulse rang all over her body like a bell. She had imagined being in his bedroom, countless times and in a countless number of ways all those years ago. And her body still reacted to it in the same way, even with a gulf of pain and dreams separating them more than ever.

She was in the Prince of Dahaar's bedroom—an intimacy that was strictly limited to his immediate family and the woman he would marry, the woman who would irrevocably belong to him.

The very thought sent a stab of pain through her middle, cooling the illicit thrill.

She clasped her nape, and rubbed it, fighting the wave of melancholy. *Ya Allah*, what madness had led her to agree to this?

A slow burn of awareness inched under her skin. She turned slowly, bracing herself for a caustic remark from those cruel lips.

Azeez stood at the doorway of the bathroom, clad only in loose white trousers that tied with fragile strings.

Sinuous heat drenched Nikhat inside out, zigzagging across a million spots, places she shouldn't be thinking of in front of him but was painfully aware of.

His shoulder blades were outlined by his lean frame. The golden olive of his skin gleamed dark against the white fabric, stretched tight over his abdomen, delineating every bone and muscle. Sparse chest hair covered dark nipples, arrowing down in a line that disappeared into those trousers. Her gaze instinctively sought the evidence of the bullet wound. Only a small length of a scar, puckered and stitched up roughly, was visible above the band of the trousers.

He didn't have a whole lot of muscle on him, and yet there was no softness to his abdomen either.

Suddenly, all she wanted was to trace the angular jut of his collarbone, rake her fingernail over his nipple, see if he felt the arc of electricity between them as strongly as she did.

She met his gaze, and something flared into life between them, contracting the space and world around them, as though shoving them both into a world of their own. His breath left him in a soft exhale and she watched as the lean chest rose and fell with it.

Liquid desire, she realized what it was, flowed through every nerve in her body, a thrill coiling her muscles. She wanted to move forward and touch him, feel the heat of his skin slide against hers, smell that intoxicating masculinity that had made her realize her own femininity for the first time.

Eight years ago, she had been naive, green, too overwhelmed by what and who he was to understand the raw awareness between them, too caught up in society's rules and her own insecurities to comprehend the power and beauty of this thing. The dark heat of his glances, the fire of his checked desire, the power with which he had leashed it so that he didn't scare her, she had never fully comprehended it. Until now.

It was not her body that had caught up, as he had mocked. It was her mind. And it reveled in the raw charge between them, reveled in the fact that she could put that feral look in his eyes.

The slight rise of his brows, the almost undetectable hint of widening of his jet-black irises—he was amused and yet it was not the eviscerating kind. He was as surprised as she was at her daring.

Coloring, she fought the instinct to look away, to hide from what he made her body feel. She had denied herself so many things. But the simple thrill of watching the Prince of Dahaar, of holding that intractable gaze without shying away, she couldn't deny herself this. It made her dizzily alive. In that moment, she could believe herself his equal.

His mouth didn't turn into a sneer, his gaze didn't mock her for her unwise audacity. He just stood there and stared at her, as though waiting to see how long she could hold it.

She could drink him in for the rest of her life. But of course, she had a job to do.

Searching for that brisk efficiency that she had become well known for among her colleagues, she waved the iPad toward him. "Since you refuse to see an actual physiotherapist, I contacted a friend of mine and downloaded some videos he recommended. Most of them are pretty easy to follow, but I have requested that Khaleef be present in case you need physical—"

He shook his head.

She instantly knew what he was saying no to. "But Khaleef can—"

"I want you."

She swallowed at the searing heat that blanketed her as he pushed off the wall and moved closer. He had said those words deliberately, she reminded herself. He was testing how far her recklessness of a few moments ago would carry her. And yet they had no less effect on her. "Fine. For this week, our goal is to get you moving again, and for you to attend a dinner with Ayaan and Princess Zohra at the end of the week. And figuring out where it is that you want to go when this is…over, and what you will be doing there."

Every muscle in his face stilled. "Where I want to go?"

"Yes. I thought about your…leaving Dahaar a little more." It was all she had done, she felt consumed by it really. This time, she was going to be here and he was going to leave.

She had long ago resigned herself to a life without him and she had accomplished far more than her wildest dreams.

Still, the thought of living in a Dahaar that didn't have him in it was a reality she had never imagined. "Ayaan won't just let you wander back into the desert. It seems more feasible that Ayaan, King Malik and Queen Fatima will—" he grimaced at the mention of his mother, and she willed herself to continue "—will let you leave if you show an interest in one of the worldwide business ventures that Dahaar invests in.

"You cannot cut them out of your life completely, Azeez. Nor are you capable of wiling away your life doing nothing. That, of all the things in the world, will kill you."

He didn't question her assumption. "I can try."

She didn't qualify that with a response. "I asked Ayaan a few questions, pretty much lied and said it would give me something to talk about with you."

"I've forgotten how meticulous you are when you set your mind to something."

"Your options are the investment house in New York, the race course in Abu Dhabi and, of course, your all-time favorite, Monaco." The last words stuck in her throat like thorns, refusing to come out.

She had developed the most violent and irrational hatred toward that place every time she had looked at the paper and read about his exploits in the year before the terrorist attack. His words that first morning had only intensified it.

A challenge glimmered in his eyes. "Is there something you would like to say, Nikhat?"

The question simmered in the air between them, like an explosive in the middle of a peaceful desert. And the slightest hint of demand from her could detonate it and crumble her carefully constructed life.

She shook her head, clinging to ignorant sanity.

Walking by his side, she adjusted her stride to match his slow one.

"I saw that—" she breathed in a deep gulp as his forearm grazed hers "—I noticed that you're not completely out of shape, but you're also obviously in pain."

He laughed, but there was no real joy in the sound. "Don't tell Ayaan. When he captured me in the desert, he knocked me off my feet and I landed on my bad hip violently. Fighting him cost me—"

"And yet you did it."

He continued as though she hadn't interrupted him. "Also, the longer—"

"The longer you sit around, drinking and throwing bottles at imaginary figures, the worse the pain gets."

"Yes. But it was too much fun, Nikhat."

She shook her head, even as a smile rose to her lips. That roguishness—it was incredible to see that still inside him. "I figure the logical step is to get you to move as much as possible every day. I inquired about a hydro-pool, but the *hammam* should do quite well for our purposes. The steam will loosen the hip joint before we do a little exercise every day. Do you know who I can contact about requesting some medical records about your bullet wound?"

"There are none."

Her mental gears checked through the list of things she had to do so rapidly that it took her a few seconds to understand. "But then who—"

"Once they realized I would be of no more use to them, the terrorist group left me in the desert to die and moved on with Ayaan, as far as I can figure. He was still valuable to them." His voice was so low, so weighed down with whatever he felt, that it raised goose bumps on her skin. "I had already lost a lot of blood. The Mijab found me, and patched up my hip the best they could. Luckily for me, I was unconscious for most of it."

Shock removed the filter from her words. "But the Mijab are not even the most advanced tribe. It's a miracle you're still standing."

Instant regret raked through her.

Because it wasn't a miracle. She had never believed in them.

Even having gone through everything he had, even weighed down by the bitterest self-loathing he seemed to be under, Azeez Al Sharif was too much a force of life to just wither away and die. The fact that he was still standing was a testament to the man's sheer willpower and nothing else.

"I like to think of it as my penance, rather."

"Penance?"

"Death would have been—it still is—too easy a punishment." His tone was matter-of-fact, as if there was no doubt about what he said. "Living my life is the harder one."

Her throat felt raw, her entire body felt raw at the quiet resignation of his words, at the emptiness in them. "Why should you have to serve penance at all? Why didn't you come back when you recovered a little?"

This was the thing that hurt and confused Ayaan the most. And her, too. The very fact that Azeez Al Sharif had chosen to stay away from Dahaar, his family, it shook the very foundations of every truth she knew.

He turned away from her, signaling an end to this conversation. "You'll have to accompany me to the *hammam*."

Whatever she had been about to say misted away. Enjoying a minute of uncensored, unwise desire she felt for him without guilt and shame was one thing, accompanying Azeez Al Sharif to what was essentially a steam room was another.

She had delivered babies, she had no false modesty or squeamishness left in her. But this was...*him*.

He halted at the door. "Unless you think what I ask is beyond the bounds of propriety and want to call the whole thing off, Dr. Zakhari?"

She fisted her hands, wanting to wipe the mockery off his face. He was constantly going to try to push her to leave. "There are servants to help you there, Azeez."

"Do you know that Ayaan had all the old servants, like

Khaleef, people who have seen me as a baby, reassigned to work in this wing?"

She frowned, remembering what her father had said. "Yes. I thought it a good security measure since you insist on not letting the people of Dahaar learn that you're alive."

His mouth set into a bitter line. "These are the same people who carried me on their shoulders in the palace, taught me how to ride a bike, celebrated with me when my father announced me Crown Prince. These are people who have known me my entire life, Nikhat. And now, when they look at me, all I see is their pity. That pity...*Ya Allah*..." He sounded tortured, his shoulders shaking with the enormity of it. She wasn't the only one who had loved him—the entire palace, all of Dahaar had worshipped their magnificent prince. "It haunts me day and night, jeers me for the mockery I have become. I hide from my parents and yet...there they are, silent witnesses to my inadequacy, to my guilt."

He turned away from her. Ayaan had truly no idea how much his brother was suffering inside these walls. "If it scares you to be around me, helping me, then say the word, *latifa*. But I will not accept help from anyone else."

That resentment would have frayed her at one time, but not anymore. Each little facet of his pain that she saw only strengthened her resolve.

Somehow, or especially because he wanted to punish her by keeping her close, he had decided she would be the one he leaned on. And even though every word from him, every moment spent with him, poked holes through her will, she still wanted to do this.

She met his gaze, striving for a casualness that she was far from feeling. "I used to feel overwhelmed and afraid and thrilled and God knows what else by you, all those years ago. I don't anymore."

His gaze swept over her cotton tunic top and leggings. "I can see that. Living away from Dahaar apparently suits you very well. You will have to change out of those clothes."

"I'm your servant, remember, not your spa buddy." That teased a smile from his mouth. "And I have already showered."

He stiffened next to her, and slowly pulled his arm away. "I know. I can smell the scent of your jasmine soap. You smell exactly like you did eight years ago." He said it as if it was a curse he was enduring. And for her, it was as if someone had sucked out the oxygen from the room. "But I'm going to need help and you will melt if you enter the *hammam* in those clothes."

CHAPTER FIVE

IN THE END, Nikhat didn't give in to his demands. At least, not completely.

The first room, which was a heat room, was an architectural marvel—a huge cavernous room with sweeping archways, its interiors made of gold marble that glittered in the billowing steam. Candles threw dim light around, just enough to spot the seats and pillars. The smell of eucalyptus filled the air, while crystal decanters in a variety of intricate shapes lay around.

Azeez lay on the marble platform in the middle, the pride of the room, his face down, his lower body covered by a thick, white towel. A concession for her.

Tendrils of her hair stuck to her forehead, her skin tingling and heating everywhere. Except to lend a hand as he settled over the marble bed, she hadn't really helped him. But suddenly, she felt the most rampant curiosity to see his wound.

Seeing it wouldn't particularly serve a purpose. And yet, she couldn't talk herself out of it. From what Ayaan had said, Azeez spoke of his wound with no one, not even a doctor. But he had spoken of it with her, in a matter-of-fact voice that glossed over the horror of it, but still he had.

She was it—his doctor, his psychiatrist, his nurse and his

friend. Had he realized what he had asked her to do? How had fate once again brought them to this point?

The timer she had set outside for thirty minutes pinged. Wiping her face on her sleeve, she made her way to him.

Bending at her waist, she placed her hands on his shoulders. His skin was like raw velvet under her hands. "Azeez, it's time to leave."

He leaned his chin on his hands, his coal-black eyes glittering with a thousand emotions in the flickering candlelight. The razor-sharp angles of his cheekbones, the strong jawline—he was a visual feast. "You have to help me up."

There was no smile on his face, but there was no bitterness, either. She wondered if he came to the same conclusion as she did.

Nodding, she pushed her sleeves back and tucked her hands under his shoulders. His muscled arms anchored around her waist, he rose up, leaning on his left side. The scent of him enveloped her, the sweat from his body mingling with hers, and he slowly slid off the marble.

She averted her gaze as he pulled on another fresh pair of loose cotton trousers. She flicked the light on and walked back to him before her courage deserted her.

"I want to see it, Azeez," she spoke in a rushed whisper. The cavernous room amplified their voices, enveloping them together.

"Not the best time to see it, *latifa*. Steam tends to do things to it," he said with a sinful curve of his mouth.

"What?" Heat scorched her cheeks as his meaning sunk in. "I'm not talking about your…your…"

"Yes, Dr. Zakhari? What precisely are you *not* talking about?" Challenge glinted in his words, his mouth tugged up at the corners.

That glimpse of his old roguish humor—it sent a blast of longing through her.

She had graduated with honors in her class. She was an ob-gyn, yes, but she had seen naked men before. And she wasn't going to let the Prince of Dahaar reduce her into a blushing twit. "Your penis, okay? That's not what I want to see. And you know what? I can also say sex, vagina, erection and—"

He threw his head back and laughed. A rich, powerful, hearty sound that brought prickling tears to her eyes, and the most painful tightness to her chest. She wanted to hear it again and again, see the flash of his teeth, feel the warmth of it steal into her. To forever be the one who made him laugh like that.

The corners of her own mouth tugged up.

"It is like you are a different woman, Nikhat. More fun, daring..." His gaze gleamed with an inferno of emotion. "*Whatever* it is that you...did in New York really agrees with you."

The unspoken question sizzled in the silence. But she didn't take his bait this time.

"I want to see your wound."

His laughter died. "There's nothing you can do for it."

Her bare feet almost slipped on the floor and she grabbed him for support. She grasped his forearms tight, refusing to let him move. "I prefer to be the person making the judgment. And as arrogant and all-knowing as you are, I'm the one with a medical degree here."

His fingers tightened on her arms, the thin cotton of her caftan no barrier to his touch. His eyes ate her up. "But I'm the Prince. I'm the one with all the power. I make the rules between us, Nikhat. I decide what I will use you for and what I won't. You seem to be under a fantastic delusion that you're as important to me as you were eight years ago. You are not. It is only your history with my family, your usefulness to me, that has you standing here. Don't mistake it as anything else."

The breath-stealing arrogance in his words bounced off her. But the fact that he belittled her presence here…she couldn't tolerate it.

In a perverse little twist, she wanted him to acknowledge that she was here because she *was* the girl he had known once, the girl he had loved once. The need for that acknowledgment burned through her even as she realized that it was dangerous.

She was standing on a precipice, and all she wanted to do was jump. "You will not steal the little I have. You've no idea what I have faced, what I still face, to be standing here in front of you without shattering into a million pieces."

His mouth, enticingly close to hers, hardened, the intensity of his focus a fierce little thing. "Why are you pushing me, *Nikhat*? Why does it matter what I think after all these years? And whatever you have faced, it was all your own doing. You chose this path, don't ask for understanding now."

"You think me heartless, you think it is easy for me being near you, seeing you in pain." She blinked at how easily the wound she closed could open again. "It is not. Every minute I spend in this palace hurts me just as much as it hurts you."

A dark smile curved his mouth and she held her breath at the stark beauty of it. He pushed a tendril of her hair behind her ear, then clasped her jaw, the rough ridges of his fingers and palm chafing against her skin. She shivered, every inch of her body focused on the minute contact. "After everything I have done, everything I have brought on myself—" his gaze caressed her eyes, her nose, her mouth, a dark fire in it "—you would think that wouldn't have given me the satisfaction it does. But I've never been magnanimous or kind or—"

"Or anything but your true self. Since you're satisfied that I'm suffering as much as you are, let me see your wound, Azeez."

"Why are you hell-bent on plunging us both into misery again? How much more do you want me to suffer?"

And just like that, he gave her back all the power he stole from her. He hated the servants seeing him like this, his brother seeing him like this, but above all, it was her presence that tortured him the most.

Why? Did he think she would be revolted? Did he not see the very strength inside him that still kept him standing there?

Suddenly, it became irrationally imperative that she learn everything he had suffered, if only to share his pain.

She would have done that much for even a friend. So she stayed silent, refusing to back away.

With a curse that punctured the air, he undid the string of his trousers and Nikhat wondered if he could hear the *thump-thump* of her heart. Breathing hard, she moved to the side to let the blazing lights overhead illuminate the small sliver of flesh he uncovered.

She breathed hard at the first sign of a violent scar— stitched up roughly, almost the width of her wrist. Closing her eyes, she laid her hand on his hip. His skin was blazing hot under her palm, the muscle clenching into rock hardness as she moved her fingers.

He stiffened but she couldn't stop herself.

A picture emerged in her mind as she moved her hand, traced the ravaged tissue, learning the breadth and length of it. She clutched her eyes closed, locking the searing heat back.

She couldn't help imagining the kind of pain he must have suffered. And following that, hope flooded through her.

She had been right. He had survived because he was Azeez Al Sharif. And if he could survive that wound, he could survive anything.

There was no smooth flesh left on the side of his hip. It was a jagged mass of muscle, the patched-up scars abrasive against her soft palm, running down his thigh. The moment her fingers fluttered lower and she felt the coarse hair of his thighs against her fingers again, it was her turn to shudder all over.

His skin here was hot and different against her palm, but the muscles rock hard.

A pulse of something else clamored between them—a heated awareness at how intimately she was touching him. He was half turned away from her, his hard body pressing into her front, his arm brushed up between her breasts, his long, rough fingers anchored around her nape.

Every inch of her came alive at the delicious pressure in all the right places. His breathing sounded harsh, too, every hard muscle that pressed into her tight with tension.

She righted his trousers, her fingers deceptively steady, as if she did this every day, as if she hadn't pulled them through an emotional firestorm goaded by a fiercely selfish desire. "Did the bullet shatter the bone?"

He sighed, as though accepting that she wasn't going to back off, and she wrapped her arms around his waist. "No. It hit the bone and dropped momentum somehow. From what I gathered from them, the Mijab were able to quickly extricate it. They took me to a hospital at the border of Zuran. A small metal joint was inserted to hold the bone together until it could grow back."

"They left it inside," she said, finally understanding the

source of his pain. "That's why it gets so stiff, why it hurts so much."

He nodded and his hands pulled her hands away from his hip. "Are we through?"

Nikhat straightened and looked away. "Here, yes. We will start stretching immediately."

She halted at the exit, her skin gleaming with vitality, her eyes blazing with piercing honesty. The fabric of her caftan stuck to her body and with her hair curling around her face, she was the most striking woman he had ever seen, and a sharp hunger, unhidden and unwelcome, yet one that made him feel fiercely alive, clawed at Azeez.

All he would have to do was close his eyes to feel the feathering touch of her fingers over his flesh, hear the sinuous whisper of her breath over his skin.

"You can't imagine what Khaleef and the others see," Nikhat said. "They see the prince who always had a kind word for them, they see the prince who remembers their name without hesitation, they see the prince whom they mourned with tears and their hearts—they do not see your limp or your scars or your guilt. And what you see is not their pity, Azeez, but their love.

"I would give anything to see my mother one more time. Think about what you're doing to yours."

His hip muscles sore, but also surprisingly limber, Azeez slid himself onto the bench in his private garden.

He had expected Nikhat to decline his invitation.

Was she as curious about him as he was about her?

The silverware tinkled as she poured him mint tea. Sitting here, as the sun streaked the sky gold and red, surrounded by lush roses, the scent of Nikhat, jasmine and something undeniably her, shouldn't have registered at all on him. Yet, as she handed him the tea and took a sweet date cake for herself, the scent of her wafted over him, teasing arousal from his beaten body.

The sensation was fierce, sharp, after so many years of feeling nothing.

He took a sip of tea and grimaced. His hip was throbbing, the muscles in his thighs and arms shaking from the strenuous stretching after four months of inactivity. "I need something stronger than this."

"No alcohol, Azeez. Not as long as you want my help."

He frowned, and yet was unable to stop smiling at the relish with which she said it. "You're enjoying this, aren't you?"

"Yes. How many women can claim Azeez Al Sharif bows to her every command?"

"None."

The cake shook in her fingers. Coloring, she put it in her mouth.

She licked a crumb from the corner of her mouth, and another kind of ache shivered in his muscles. He felt incredibly hungry for a taste of her mouth, for a taste he had been denied for so long. And the fact that he hadn't touched a woman since the attack, the six years of celibacy, had little bearing on his desire for her.

The delicious tightening of his muscles, the coils of heat spreading like wildfire through him, they were all because of the woman who had boldly traced his scars with her hand even as her breath had hitched in her throat.

She was such a mixture of strength and vulnerability, of caring and indifference, every word from her a contradiction to her actions, he felt as if he would never understand her.

For as long as he could remember, she had been the one woman who hadn't cowed in front of him, who hadn't thrown herself at him, the one woman who had always spoken her mind, pushed him into broadening his.

Whether it was philosophy they had discussed, or the state of education for women in Dahaara, he had never been the Prince of Dahaar with her. Her answers, her arguments, they had held a piercing honesty that had been as compelling as her artlessness. For all his impulsive and passionate nature, he hadn't fallen in love with her overnight.

He had fallen in love over a period of ten years, or even more, maybe—slowly, unknowingly, tempered into it like water chipping away the surface of a rock, molding it to its will. One morning, he had woken up in his hotel suite after a night of raucous partying and suddenly wondered what she would say if she saw him then, what words she would use to skewer him, and with a fire in his blood, he had realized he had fallen in love with her, that he had found his future queen, that nothing in the world would stop him from making her his.

Except he hadn't realized the iron will of the woman herself.

And when she left, she had not just broken his heart or dented his ego, though it had been that, too. She had ripped away a piece of him that had belonged only to her and taken it with her, had left a terrifying emptiness that he'd had no idea how to fill.

Bitter jealousy vented through his veins as he studied her. Because now, now she was even better than before, now she was magnificent, everything he had imagined she would grow into and more.

Age had only refined her beauty, and from the little he remembered of when she had held on to him in the *hammam*, she was in incredibly good shape. But even better than physical beauty, she had seen the world, she had held her own in a foreign country and she had achieved everything she had set her mind to. And he...he was barely a man.

His curiosity wasn't going to simmer down quietly. He didn't even pretend he could control his emotions, or himself, when it came to her. All he could do was limit the damage to himself and her.

This...might have begun with the debilitating need to hurt her, but it wasn't anymore. In a cruel twist of fate, which didn't even surprise him, she had become the only way out for him.

"Why didn't you marry?"

She stilled, her hand midway to her mouth. He saw her fingers shake as she put the last piece of the date cake on the small silver plate. She made a show of wiping her fingers. Buying herself time, he realized. *Why?* "Are you expecting an honest answer?"

He frowned, trying to make sense of her, of everything he knew about her, of everything she had done eight years ago. Because as much as he wanted to consign it to the back of his mind, the fact that she was here in Dahaar, seeing him through this, it had to mean something.

Whether he wanted to face it when his life was already in such turmoil, he didn't know. "When have I ever asked you for anything but the truth? You're successful, you're beautiful, and as your father mentioned, you're not bound by Dahaaran traditions or customs. So why are you still single?"

She wrapped her arms around herself, her shoulders unsteady.

His heart slammed hard against his rib cage. "Or do you have a boyfriend tucked away somewhere, Dr. Zakhari, just waiting for your signal to show up?"

Something moved across her face—defiance, a challenge. Her spine locked, her mouth settling into a stubborn line that he detested. "And if I did?"

He gripped the armrests of the chaise, perverse fury filling his veins. "I have no wish to see you and your lover parade through my palace."

She leaped from her seat as though propelled toward him by a desert storm. She bent toward him, bringing her face close to his, her gaze blazing with resolve. An expression he had never seen on her before—a reckless willfulness, danced in it. And he felt the strangest little thrill gripping his insides. "I thought I didn't have to choose between my career and personal life."

She was taunting him, she was relearning what effect she had on him and testing it. And yet, he rose to meet it.

He clasped her cheek. "Do not pretend to misunderstand me or be so reckless as to challenge me, Nikhat.

"You are the woman I loved once, the woman I chose for my future queen, the woman I wanted to give birth to the future heir of Dahaar. Everything's changed in eight years, hasn't it? But the thought of you with another man, the image of any man possessing your body, staking his claim on you, it will always reduce me into a savage that would make my marauding ancestors proud.

"What I consider mine once, I would not share it, even in thought. So unless you want to add to my long list of sins, Nikhat, tuck your lover away until I leave."

He pushed himself to his knees with a savage force that sent a shock wave through his leg. He could not bear to look at her, he could not bear to look inside himself. He had thought after all these years, after everything that had happened, there was nothing left in him that would react to her, and yet, there still was.

He had wrought destruction on himself, on his family, he was directly responsible for the death of his sister and for the atrocities his brother had suffered, because of how broken, how reckless he had become when Nikhat had left him.

"I was engaged three years ago, to a colleague," she said behind him, and he halted. The very thought crept into his head and taunted him.

That she was telling him this was not to assuage his pride or to balance the scales between them. That she was offering a piece of truth was something else. Something that stole into him with an insidious inevitability that filled ice in his veins. But he would not accept it, he could not go down that path ever again, and certainly not with her. "But it didn't work out."

"Why not?" he said, the question falling from his lips before he could stop it.

She shrugged, and he instinctively knew whatever she was going to say was not the truth. "He broke it off a week before the wedding, changed his mind about what he wanted in life." Pain streaked across her gaze. "I am not… made for relationships."

Without waiting for a response, she left him in the garden, his mind roiling with every little word she had spoken.

You have no idea what I have faced, what I still face, to be standing in front of you without shattering into a million pieces.

Maybe he didn't and, for once, Azeez was thankful for his ignorance. Because the rate at which they were going, it wouldn't be long before they ripped each other to pieces.

With a self-preservation instinct that had kept him alive until now, he realized he didn't want to face any more truths.

CHAPTER SIX

SHE HAD NOT come for two days.

Two long days that Azeez had spent wondering why he cared and then eviscerating himself for the fact that he did. First he had had to check if Princess Zohra was in good health.

She was fine, the Princess had informed him with a ferocious glint in her eyes, obviously surprised that he had cared enough to check for himself.

But there was something about riling the fierce princess that loosened the chain of guilt around his neck. She had not only glared at him but had also had the temerity to warn him that Nikhat was under her protection.

Before informing him finally that Nikhat hadn't seemed well yesterday morning. And the thought of Nikhat all alone in the palace, because he was sure she wouldn't have asked anyone for help, had finally dragged him out of his suite.

He stood outside her suite now, staring at the dark wooden door with its intricate designs. They had finally settled down into a sort of routine.

He visited the *hammam* in the morning, followed by a strenuous bout of physiotherapy—in which the madwoman drove him like the very devil intent on punishing him for all his sins. Sometimes she would stay and have lunch with him. They ate in silence—not completely awkward. But not pleasant, either, as though they were still reeling from the words they had thrown at each other two days before.

He had caught her casting puzzled looks at him, seen the way she caught herself when she was irked by his politeness, astonished that he was even capable of it with her.

Now, standing outside her door, he questioned his sanity again. He needed to treat her like any other employee, any other servant that his brother had. Let her come find him whenever she was well and offer him an excuse.

But he couldn't stop wondering about what would cause the ruthlessly efficient woman to be absent.

He pushed the doors and stepped in. It was early evening, but the French doors to her suite were still open, and brought a chill inside.

Frowning, he closed them. The suite bore her stamp clearly. The subtle scent of jasmine and her skin, wafted over him, knuckling him in the gut, unlocking a million memories inside his head.

There were medical journals, an iPad and a scarf dangling on the table in the lounge. An old framed picture of her with her three younger sisters sat next to the scarf.

A low, keening moan came from the bedroom. He turned instantly, a slow chill racing up his spine. He pushed the bedroom door open.

She lay in the middle of the bed, dressed in loose white pajamas that hung low on her hips and a loose cotton tunic in faded yellow. Her thick, wavy hair fanned out against the white sheets shone like copper-gold silk. Lying on her side, her arms clasped her belly so tight that her knuckles showed white. She moaned again and this time, the pain in the sound made the hair on his arms stand.

He got onto the bed slowly, making sure not to put too much weight on his right hip. She looked so pale, the golden hue of her usual color all but gone. Her eyes were red and swollen. That she had shed tears was a fact he couldn't believe even when presented with evidence.

Nikhat never cried. He remembered the day when her mother had died. She had been twelve. And yet Azeez only remembered her resolve to be strong for her younger sisters. Shifting closer to her, he pushed the sweat-slicked hair back from her forehead. His breath left him in a long exhale, thankful that her skin wasn't burning up.

She stiffened suddenly, as if a hot poker was lancing her next to him, and then shivered uncontrollably as another wave of pain hit, he realized. He clasped her fingers with his tightly, willing her to draw strength from him. He felt the tremble slowly fade from her body, heard her breath leave in a jagged exhale. The whimper of relief that accompanied it caught the breath in his throat. "Nikhat, *ya habeebiti*, look at me," he said. Watching her like this, he felt powerless and, at the same time, gripped with a fierce determination to see her through it.

She jerked her head back, her gaze flying to him. He thought she would stiffen and move away, demand to be released, tell him she didn't need his comfort.

"Azeez?"

"Yes, Nikhat."

Fresh tears welled up in her beautiful eyes, and he felt as if someone had kicked him in the gut. She scooted closer to him on the bed, and her arms went tight around his waist. "It hurts, Azeez. So much. Every time that wave comes, it feels like I will die." Her tears leaked out of her eyes, drawing wet tracks onto her cheeks.

He wiped them with a shaking hand, his heart jammed in his throat. "Why, in God's name, haven't you summoned help? I'll have them fly a specialist in, anything you need. Is it some kind of fever, an infection?"

She shook her head and hid her face in his abdomen. But

not before he caught a shadow of something in her eyes. He sunk his fingers into her thick hair, rubbing her scalp in a soothing manner. "I'm going to get my period soon," she said with no hesitation that belied the way she hid her face.

And suddenly he remembered how she used to disappear every month for a few days, and shy away when he asked her about it. Knowing that it would only make her retreat from her, he had never pressed her about it. "Have they always been so painful?" he asked now. It galled him to imagine her suffering like this every month for so many years.

And he thought he knew everything there was about pain.

She nodded, and her nose tickled his abdomen. He tightened his muscles, willing his body not to betray its automatic reaction to her nearness. "As far as I can remember."

"So what do we do?"

"I have learned to manage it with medication and exercise, and breathing techniques. It's so stupid, but I…forgot to renew my medication on time before I left. It's on its way from New York. Should be delivered tomorrow morning."

"And until then?" he said, his throat dry.

"Until then, I just bear it the best I can. It's really bad only for a few hours," she whispered in a small voice. He pulled himself up until he was sitting a little straighter. Her palm moved from his abdomen to his chest, and his heart thundered like a wild animal under her tentative fingers. The thin cotton of his tunic was no barrier to the feel of her touch.

"Azeez?"

Her breath feathered over his neck, the scent of her drugging arousal into his blood. He felt engulfed by her, as if he was standing on shifting sands that could pull him under any minute.

"Yes, *habeebi?*" he finally said through a throat as dry as the desert.

"Will you stay with me tonight?"

He froze. She had never asked him for anything when he would have given her the world. No matter, she didn't have the right now, the saner part of him argued back.

"Please, Azeez."

"You will hate me tomorrow for seeing you like this, *Nikhat*. You have never liked sharing your pain or grief," he said, remembering what a stoic little girl she had always been. It was that very strength that he had found endlessly fascinating.

But circumstances had forced her to become like that and she had never complained. He had watched her learn to cook and manage her sisters at a young age, ecstatically happy that she was being allowed to do the one thing she most wanted—to study by Amira's side. It had taken very little for her to be happy.

She sighed and hugged him tighter. Her chest grazed his, the soft push of her breasts against his muscles was more torture than he could take. His blood sang at the pleasure, but it was seeing her like this—pain-ridden and vulnerable—that tightened his gut.

"I won't, Azeez." He heard her sniffle. "The strange thing is, I could never hate you whatever you do or say. You…have this power over me. I've always considered myself a strong woman, I *am* a strong woman. But when it comes to you, I…" She exhaled, and burrowed closer to him.

Eviscerated by her admission, he chanced a look at her. She looked drowsy, her eyelids swollen. "Did you take any painkillers, Nikhat?"

"Hmm…" she whispered, blinking. "Yes. These just take longer to kick in. Will you stay with me?" Her lush mouth curved into a smile. "Can we also pretend that you don't hate me for a few hours?"

He closed his eyes and wrapped his arms around her. She was so soft all over, her fragility a complete contrast to the steely core of the woman.

He had never held a woman close like this, never offered comfort. Except with Nikhat, he had only ever wanted and taken only physical release from women.

"You make the most outrageous demands of your Prince, Dr. Zakhari," he said, holding her that way costing him. "But I will try."

She melted into him with a sigh. And the satisfaction in that sound, coupled with the way she held him, hard and unrelenting, sent ripples of powerful hunger through him. "I like it when you call me that, even as you shred me to pieces doing it."

He moved his fingers over her arm in a slow ripple. "I'm the one who paid the price for that degree, *ya habeebiti*. Of course it sounds special when I say it."

He felt her smile just before she gripped him hard again.

Her body writhed against his, her hand bunching over her lower belly, as though to fight that pain. She made a long, gasping sound with her throat and stiffened against him.

Ya Allah, what he wouldn't give to take that pain away from her. Clutching her tightly against him, Azeez held her hard. He couldn't tear his gaze away from her, couldn't uncouple himself from her pain, from her strength.

Just as he heard her breath even out, something inside him, something that he had no control over asked the question. "Nikhat, this condition you have, does it have a name?"

"Stage four endometriosis."

His mind latched onto the word, and Azeez knew it would never leave him alone.

Your Prince.

He had referred to himself as her prince. It had a very nice ring to it, Nikhat decided, snuggling languorously into the solid warmth of his body.

He was hers, the man who had promised to make every silly little dream of hers come true.

Against all odds, Azeez bin Rashid Al Sharif, the magnificent and breathtaking Crown Prince of Dahaar had somehow fallen in love with her. He had laughed all her doubts away when she had said she was not suited to be queen, he had forsaken all other women, the prince who had women throughout the world falling over him, for her, had promised her that he would always love her and keep her happy.

She would have to be the queen, of course. But with him by her side, Nikhat felt she could rule the whole universe, if that's what was required.

An echo of a dull ache spread through her lower belly, and suddenly all her dreams shattered into a million pieces around her. It was the bitterest kind of reality to wake up to, but it was her reality, her life.

Her happiness, she had realized, hadn't been in his power *or* hers.

Opening her eyes, she saw that she was coiled around Azeez like a vine. Delicious warmth spread under her skin. Licking her dry lips, she glanced at the bedside digital alarm clock. It was half past two. The bed lamp was still on.

She was lying on her left side, her legs tangled with Azeez's, her arm tight around his hips. She gasped as she realized how hard she was holding him, pressing her left hand into his damaged hip. She was about to jerk it back when he grasped her wrist and held it there. "That pressure feels good, *habeebi*."

She stilled, a thousand different voices clamoring to be heard inside her head. And yet, not a single one of them was even a token protest. She only felt exhilaration, only the utmost lethargy. Not shame, or disbelief or any such thing.

Azeez Al Sharif, even when he considered himself a cripple, was a perfect specimen of masculinity that would induce knee-jerking reaction in any woman. And the intimacy of waking up next to him like this was like a drug that filled her with inexplicable longing.

What she felt, coiled against him, was healthy, thrilling, one of the few things that validated her femininity. After the last day of pain that was a reminder of everything she was not, the warm languor in her muscles, the slow burn of desire, she welcomed it wholeheartedly.

He was hard against her and warm. He smelled the way he always did—of sandalwood and exquisite heat and dark, sinful promises. She sucked in a deep breath, savoring the scent of him. Against the onslaught of those sensations, the dull ache in her lower belly was almost negligible.

Feeling his gaze on her, she glanced up. His features looked strained, dark shadows under his eyes. Had he slept with his torso leaning against the headboard? She made to move, but his arm around her didn't budge. "I'm sorry. You must have been very uncomfortable."

He shrugged, his gaze devouring her with a quiet intensity that should have alarmed her. Instead, it swathed her with an electrifying thrill. "I don't remember the last time I slept through the night anyway. It was only a few hours. And every time, I tried to make myself more comfortable, you held on so tight that I was afraid to hurt you, or even worse, wake you up when it looked like you finally had some relief."

She felt color swamp her cheeks. "Thank you for staying with me. I have forgotten how awful it gets."

"And when you take these medications that you are waiting for?"

"It's quite different because they are pure hormones, they make my body…" She blinked, trying to backtrack slowly. "The pain is quite manageable coupled with regular exercise and deep breathing."

"All those trips you made in Dahaara and then overseas?"

She winced, remembering those trips with her father's sister. The despair that she would never find relief, it was the thing she remembered most. "I had already seen every doctor I could in Dahaar. None of them ever gave me a conclusive diagnosis. Just kept telling me it was normal, that I had to just cope with it.

"That pain…it would cripple me every month.

"My father—" she cleared her throat "—I used to get so angry with him. My mother was already gone when the pains started and he…" She felt the force of Azeez's anger and released hers. "He…couldn't talk about it with me, wouldn't even come near me. He was too traditional for that. But he didn't give up on me, either. He sent me to New York with a family friend. Someone recommended a…specialist there. She ran a lot of tests. And within a week, she recommended these drugs and other measures."

"This is why you became an ob-gyn?"

She nodded, glad to be able to share at least half the truth. "No one should have to go through this kind of pain for so many years. I want to bring more awareness to the condition. It's already a hard subject for a young girl to talk about. Then when someone does have the courage to speak up, she is told again and again to just live with it, that it is natural. Nothing about this pain is bearable."

His fingers tightened over her arms and she clasped them with hers. When he spoke, his voice was low, gravelly and full of pride. Her heart sang at it. "You will succeed, Nikhat. I have no doubt. Draw up a proposal. Vet out some experts in the field that would like to work in Dahaar. Think of every resource that you might need and put it on that proposal. You have my complete backing and my personal fortune at your disposal."

Tears prickled at the back of her eyes, and this time, she didn't stem them. They were not borne of pain or grief. Those first couple of years after she had left, being amongst strangers, thinking he was forever gone, she had lost her faith, doubted her ability to do what she had wanted.

The pride shining in his eyes felt like her true prize. He thought she was strong, but hadn't she always measured her words, her actions, through his eyes, his honor?

"And here I assumed you were an impoverished, deadbeat prince," she said, laughing through her tears. "I have to remember to be nice to you."

His mouth curved into a smile, the long sweep of his lashes mesmerizingly beautiful as his gaze widened. "Charming the prince for money? Very disappointing of you, Dr. Zakhari," he said with mock insult, and she laughed some more.

Giving in to the urge that beat at her relentlessly, she clasped his cheek. Traced his jawline with her thumb, the stubble on it rasping against her skin. She heard his breath hitch as she moved her finger to his mouth, saw the warning flash in his eyes, but she couldn't stop.

His upper lip had a perfect bow shape to it, while the lower one had an indulgent lushness.

She had wanted to touch him for so long, without shyness, without being consumed by her insecurities. Just for how good it made her feel, just for how right he felt. He clasped her wrist, halting her. "Nikhat? Do not—"

She jerked herself up to a sitting position, traced the seam of his lower lip. His breath hissed out, the cushion of his lip soft and warm against her finger.

Her own breath rushing out of her, she slanted her head and touched her mouth to his.

He became incredibly still. If not for the rough rumbling sound he made in his throat, she would have thought him a block of marble, a hot one. Anchoring her hands on his shoulders, she pressed little kisses along the seam of his lower lip, along every inch of his perfect, bow-shaped upper lip. His lips were soft and rough at the same time, sending sparks of heat careening to every tip of her body.

Impatient for more, she licked his lower lip when he exhaled a jagged breath, and then tugged it with her teeth.

And he exploded like a volcano that had finally reached its erupting point. His hands found her hips and pulled her toward him so hard that her breasts slammed against his chest, and she fell onto him sideways. His fingers crept into her hair, held her tightly as he devoured her mouth with his.

He had kissed her once all those years ago. She had been avoiding him, going out of her way to minimize seeing the dark and blindingly beautiful prince she had foolishly fallen in love with.

And one afternoon, he had cornered her in the library where Amira and she usually studied, locked the door behind him and kissed her.

It had lasted maybe be a few seconds before she had pushed him away, shaken and overwhelmed at the maelstrom of sensations it had stirred within her. If that had been a minor tremor in an earthquake, what he did to her today with his mouth was a hurricane.

The scent of him filled her breath, his muscles digging and shifting against her body.

He nibbled her lower lip with a growl that gave her goose bumps, and a lick of heat swept through her, waking up every nerve ending. With his tongue, he laved her, pushing for entrance, and she let him in with a moan.

He licked at the interior of her mouth, tangled with her tongue with such erotic intent that her breasts felt heavy, and a different kind of ache began in her lower belly. Their teeth clanged and scraped, their tongues tangled. She was awash in such sensations, such mind-bending delirium, that it took her a moment to realize he had ripped open her tunic in the front. Her nipples tightened into needy knots as his gaze, hot and erotic, fell on her breasts clad in a lacy black bra.

Her gaze flew to his, and held, a storm of desire gleaming in his. Never wavering from her, he moved his fingers to the seam of lace. The moment his fingers touched her flesh, everything inside Nikhat shuddered, gathered behind that contact, waiting for more.

Because, God, she wanted more.

Twin bands of color streaked his cheekbones, his breath sounding swift and harsh.

Anticipation coiled in every muscle, a feverish heat broke out on her skin.

His face taut with desire, he slowly set her away from him. Nikhat felt his retreat as sharply as if he had slapped her. "So I take it this…this sexual independence is another by-product of your relationship with your colleague?"

She laughed, hiding her unease at the swift change in conversation, and pulled the mass of her hair away from her neck and tied it up with her scarf. His gaze darkened, the stamp of lust on his face flooded her with utter satisfaction. He might hate her, but he desired her still. Even acknowledging that it was an utterly useless response, Nikhat reveled in it. "I am a doctor, and I am thirty years old, Azeez. I don't find anything shameful about sexual pleasure."

His fingers tightened over her arm, he dragged her until she hit the wall of his chest. The savage snarl of his mouth, instead of frightening her, thrilled her. "That's quite a shame, isn't it? Because eight years ago, I was on my knees, begging for a single kiss. I didn't touch another woman for two years because I wanted you."

Pushing away his resisting arms, she burrowed into his warmth. So many regrets and not a single one that she could explain. "You have no idea how much I regretted it."

"What did you regret?"

She looked up at him, knowing that, once again, she was going to disappoint him. "Not making love with you. There were so many nights that I dreamed you were next to me, kissing me, touching me, so many moments when I wished…" She moved out of his reach, bitterness swiftly adding a chill to the air. "And in the morning, I would see another article about you with a new woman. The Prince of Dahaar sowing his wild oats in Monaco, leaving every single party with a new woman. What had they called you, the insatiable prince?" But still, she hadn't been able to help herself, she hadn't been able to stop herself from dreaming about him.

He frowned, his gaze drilling into her. "You walked away. I offered you everything."

"So, of course, that means you can sleep with countless women, doesn't it?" The words slipped out on a wave of bitter jealousy that scoured through her. She had no right to ask these questions. There was no need to add more bitterness to this fire between them. But she couldn't stop. "Tell me, Azeez. Was it so easy to forget me, to wipe every thought of me from your mind, from your life?"

And the moment the words spilled out, she wanted to pull them back. Shivering at the slow dawning of anger in his eyes, she clasped her hand over his mouth.

He pulled her hand from his mouth slowly. "Afraid to hear the answer, *ya habeebiti*? Would you prefer it if I lie?"

There was no point in asking him to lie. Because he would not. The Prince of Dahaar never lied, not for his sake, not for hers.

"You think it was about hurting you, about proving that you were nothing to me?" His soft words landed on her like fiery lashes, burning into her skin.

"Every woman I slept with, I was only cheapening myself. Their faces faded one after the other, the pleasure I found with them transient and shameful...I would wake up in the middle of the night, tangled in bare limbs, sick to my stomach." The set of his mouth matching the blazing disgust in his eyes, he shuddered. "In my eyes, what you didn't want was worth nothing to me. I went on a rampage, wondering how I would fill the void, becoming reckless in pursuit of relief, raining down destruction on myself and..."

The shiver in his hands as he ran them through his hair, the utter loathing in his eyes, it was like a slap to Nikhat. How selfish and destructive was she to ask that question?

He slipped out of the bed and walked away. At the door, he turned back. "Let Princess Zohra know if you continue to be unwell. She should be able to arrange anything you need."

The silence of the suite bore down upon her as Azeez closed the door behind him. Nikhat pulled the sheets toward herself and they bore the scent of him. She clutched it to herself.

What you didn't want was worth nothing to me.

Those words lanced through her, leaving invisible, permanent marks on her. She had asked for it and he had given it to her, shredding the last thread of lies she had held on to all these years.

Telling herself that he had instantly cast her out of his mind after she left Dahaar, reading about his exploits almost greedily during that first year, she had found a kind of solace in the fact that he had moved on, fooled herself that she had been nothing but a novelty at a distance.

All of them delusions she had set in place to protect herself.

Now his words left her nothing to hide behind.

He had loved her, by his own confession, he had plunged himself into a reckless lifestyle to fill the void she had left... She hugged her knees, the pain of her body paling in comparison to the pain his words had unleashed.

Guilt tightened like an iron chain around her throat, choking her.

Staying here after learning that he was alive—what had she been thinking? How had she forgotten what it had cost her last time to walk away? How had she forgotten how strong this pull between them was?

Throwing the existence of her relationship, even a failed one, in his face, challenging him with her presence every step of the way, giving in to the urge to kiss him, to touch him, playing with his emotions and her own, there was no excuse for her behavior. When had she become so reckless as to tempt fate again, so selfish as to satisfy her own twisted sense of self?

She needed to remember why she was here, and what Azeez had already been through.

Learning that she might never conceive, accepting her inability to be the woman he needed her to be had wrecked her. For months, she had thought herself less than a woman, her entire identity as a woman fracturing because she might not be able to give the man she loved the heirs he needed. And in the end, her love for him had asked for a sacrifice of her own happiness.

She had, somehow, survived through it and built a life for herself. She couldn't risk all that again.

CHAPTER SEVEN

A WEEK LATER, Nikhat arrived at the breakfast hall in the morning, and came to a halt, her heart thudding.

Azeez and Ayaan stood on either side of the table, their hands fisted, their expressions similarly battling fury and more. Princess Zohra was standing by Ayaan's side, her gaze flitting between the brothers.

A needle dropped into the room would have sounded like an explosion.

Nikhat's gaze invariably went to Azeez. And first thing that came to her mind was how good he looked even as his face was currently wreathed in tension.

He wore a snowy-white cotton tunic that was open to his chest, the startling white of the fabric contrasting against his sunburned throat and face. His jaw shaved, the unhealthy pallor that had been there when she had first arrived was gone.

And his jet-black eyes had the biggest difference.

With each passing day, the arrogance, the confidence that had made him, came back.

Heat swamped her, but she couldn't look away before stealing a look at that sensuous mouth. It had been just a kiss.

But it had started a fire in her that couldn't be quenched, whatever she did. Not that there had been a hint of interest from him again.

His withdrawal was so absolute that there was no need for her to worry that she would weaken again. Not when he looked at her as if she was the plague he was determined to avoid. There were no more cutting remarks, no allusions to past or present, nothing but a polite, entirely painful, coldness.

Taking a deep breath, she looked around the room, the tension in it sinking heavily into her shoulders. "Is something wrong?"

Nerves at breaking point, Azeez turned toward Nikhat and was instantly assaulted by the taste of her mouth, her soft curves that had fit so perfectly against his. Desire slumbered in his blood, a constant companion that mocked him.

This seesaw of emotions every time he looked at her was the last thing he needed in his life right now. He had to get away from the palace, from her, from his brother. He had to do something useful or go crazy.

"I proposed a trip to the desert and my brother is threatening to lock me up and throw away the key."

She paled, her angular features even more stark. Dark circles hung under her bright eyes. For once, he didn't feel the sadistic pleasure that she wasn't handling this any better than him. "Why?"

"Because, as you are well aware, I'm going mad sitting here doing nothing."

"I have to run this country, Azeez. I don't have time to come looking for you nor an answer for Mother if you disappear again. You can't do this to her again."

Azeez flinched, even as he deserved his words. How did he explain to his brother how useless he felt here, even as every single palace matter around him seeped into his blood? His mind, not drenched by alcohol, and his body making slow progress toward less pain, he needed to get out.

He chose his words carefully, the very idea that had come to him this morning filling him with renewed energy. But he didn't want his brother to latch onto it and use it as weapon to bind Azeez to Dahaar permanently.

"Khaleef said there have been problems with communications to the Sheikh of Zuran."

Just as he expected, a light came on in Ayaan's eyes. "I think Khaleef needs a lesson in protocol, and a reminder about who the Crown Prince of Dahaar is now."

"I'm still the bloody Prince of —" Azeez gripped the back of his chair, fighting the urge to knock off that knowing smile from his brother's lips. A lifetime of duty and privilege in his blood was hard to get rid of. "Is it true or not?"

"Yes," Ayaan said, moving to the window. "I persuaded the Sheikh Asad to sign a treaty four months ago, along with Zohra's father, about better protection along the borders for all three nations. Now he's not responding, nor is the High Council of Zuran." Ayaan ran a hand along his nape. "I don't like the silence on their side."

"That's why it's imperative that I go."

"I don't understand."

His brother had truly become everything he needed to be king. Azeez knew Ayaan was only acting ignorant to force him to put the proposal into words. But anything was better than being stuck here, visiting the past in a relentless loop. "I have contacts, Ayaan. How do you think I gathered the information that I fed you before you brought me here? I can have them dig out information on what's going on in Zuran for you. Sheikh Asad was always a thorn in father's side, too."

The silence that met his statement was more deafening than an explosion. And it pulled his already stretched patience thin.

The restlessness inside him grated at him. He had never in his life been without purpose like this. And he had to find one, first a temporary one and then a permanent one.

"I don't know that you're physically up to—"

"Of course I am. I survived without you or your doctors for six years. I came back from a wound that tore my hip apart. I remained sane as blood left my body remembering Amira's face and yours." Azeez held his brother's gaze, hating him in that moment.

"This is the one thing where I can do something to help, instead of being trapped here in this palace," he said through gritted teeth, willing his brother to understand him. "I'll never be anything but a prisoner inside these walls, Ayaan. When will you see that?"

A tightness inched into his face as Ayaan studied him. "Fine," he finally said, his mouth compressed into a thin line. "Nikhat will accompany you then."

"No."

The denial, spat out at the same time by Nikhat and he, reverberated around the vast hall.

Both Ayaan and Zohra cast them looks, confusion and concern ringing in their gazes. "No choice for either of you," Ayaan announced.

Azeez clicked his jaw shut, fighting for control over his temper. "Fine." He turned toward Nikhat. "We leave at dawn tomorrow morning."

Nikhat shivered as Azeez moved past her, and the heat from his body beckoned her. But she couldn't let him pass without doing her duty, without asking the question that she needed to. She clasped his wrist just as he turned. "You missed your sessions two days in a row."

His fingers landed on hers before she could blink, his mouth bared in a snarl. But whatever he had thought never came out. "No. I didn't. I just took Khaleef with me," he whispered in a low voice that pinged over her bare nape.

But his unguarded expression told her everything he didn't say. He had been getting increasingly short-tempered and restless these past few days, as though struggling against invisible chains.

And just like that the pieces clicked into place. She loosened her grip on him, and he left.

She had heard the quiet whispers among the older servants about the charity function tomorrow, the annual presentation for the educational trust that was set up in her name...

How had she forgotten?

She had looked at her calendar as she always did, this morning, too, without a second's thought.

"Would you like to explain, Nikhat?"

Nikhat braced herself and turned to face Ayaan. "There's nothing to exp—" It was the first time she saw real fury in his copper-colored gaze.

"What in God's name did my brother mean about always being a prisoner?"

She could just tell him it was nothing or she could tell him the truth and hope he would begin to understand. Because it was never going to be easy to accept. Thinking Azeez had been dead was one thing. Knowing he was alive somewhere in the world, but away from Dahaar, would be a special kind of torture. On every one of them. "He needs a breather, Ayaan. From you, from the palace, from everything that's been going on."

Princess Zohra bristled next to Ayaan. "He's the one who's—"

Nikhat met the princess's gaze full on. "You do not know what he suffers, Princess. Believe me, none of us do." Only after the words were out did she realize how defiant she sounded.

Ayaan leveled a thoughtful look at her. "Say what's on your mind, Nikhat. Without hesitation."

"It's Amira's birthday tomorrow."

Ayaan looked as if she had struck him. Zohra's hand found his and tightened. That's what Azeez needed too. And despite her resolve to keep everything utterly professional between them, Nikhat realized she couldn't leave Azeez alone. Not tomorrow, of all days.

"He…" She ran a shaking hand over her face, struggling to find the words. "He's suffering, Ayaan, in the palace. He's trying, for your sake, but—"

Ayaan shook his head, refusing to let her finish. "You promised me, Nikhat. You gave me your word—"

"Yes, to help *him*," she burst out.

She held his gaze, saw the threat that rose to his lips.

Fear rattled inside her. She was antagonizing the future King, the man who could crash her dreams in Dahaar with one word. And for all his kindness, she had no doubt Ayaan would do *anything* to keep his brother close.

But even with her future hanging in the balance, she couldn't back down from her promise to Azeez. She took a deep breath, wondering why she even put up a fight with herself. Nothing was ever simple, ever free of emotions when it came to Azeez Al Sharif. "I'm sorry I didn't make this clear sooner. But Azeez will always have my loyalty first."

"Then you seal your fate along with his."

"It would seem so." Nikhat nodded at him and Princess Zohra and left the hall with her head held high.

He was creeping through his own palace like a thief of the night, but he had left himself no choice. Behind him, the deserted corridor was bathed in yellow light from the lamps. He chanced a look at the courtyard, and the utter silence in there, in this whole wing, jeered him.

Azeez leaned his head against the closed door and struggled to get air into his lungs. He couldn't hide forever from this. He nodded at Khaleef to open the door, and another figure appeared in the corridor and joined him.

Instead of recoiling, as everything inside him was wont to do, he let Nikhat lace her fingers with his. He didn't question how she knew that he was standing outside Amira's door at the first light of dawn, or how terrified he was of facing this day.

The palace was not the same without his sister's laughter. But he had to apologize to her and he wanted to do it here, in her suite where she had laughed and cried, where she had lived such a vibrant life before his recklessness had shortened it.

He pushed the door and stepped in. The scent of Amira as he remembered—roses and something sweet—hit him in the gut. His knees buckled and tears clogged his throat, and he let them fall.

As Nikhat turned on the light, he walked around the huge chamber where everything had been left as it was before her death. Her jewelry lay haphazardly on the dark dresser, her nightstand overflowing with novels.

How he wished he could change his reckless behavior all those years ago, how he wished he had realized sooner that Amira and Ayaan had stayed back to confront him that night in the desert, how he wished he had taken the bullet that had claimed her life…

Her arm clamped around his middle, Nikhat hugged him tightly. And for once, he couldn't find it in him to push her or the comfort she offered away. They stood like that for several minutes, drowning in memories but anchoring each other.

"Do you remember the time you complained that your prized bottle of single-malt whiskey had disappeared?"

Frowning, he nodded.

"You raised hell about it, turned the palace upside down. For so many days, I remember seeing the palace staff whispering, scared to tell you that they hadn't found it. It was like martial law had been declared in the palace."

He turned toward her. "What are you talking about, Nikhat?"

"Amira paid one of the maids to steal it." She made a choking noise with her throat and stepped back as he advanced on her. Her hands up in front of her, her head shaking, her mouth wreathed in smiles.

It made her face light up, reminding him of a carefree time. "I saved it for so long, I…"

"I begged her not to, Azeez. It was the vilest thing I ever tasted in my life. I mean, after the first few sips, I couldn't even stomach it. I told her we should return it, but by that time you had guards outside your wing like the crown jewels were lost. We had to pour the stuff down the toilet and I smuggled the bottle out of the—"

His mouth fell open. "That was eighteenth-century whiskey that my father gave me." He suddenly remembered something else. "She was sick that next day. Did she—?"

Nikhat was openly laughing now. "She had a whole glass of it, and she called me a coward."

That sounded very much like his sister, always getting into trouble, always trying to find new ways to defy their mother's rules.

"She was so drunk, Azeez. You should have seen her. She used to mimic you…you know, the way you walked and talked, the way you would blush every time you saw Queen Fatima's friend's daughter. She was hilarious that night. I always wished I had been more like her. So full of life, treating every day as if it was an adventure.

"Her life might have been short, but she lived it to the full. Amira had been so happy that she was going to marry the man she loved, she couldn't stop smiling. And you, you had made it all possible, Azeez."

And then he had led her to her death before it had come true.

She put her arm around his. "She was so angry with me when I left that she refused to see me when I came to say goodbye. I miss her so much, Azeez."

Nodding, Azeez pulled Nikhat close, the grief inside him tempering in that moment. "Thank you for bringing back fond memories for me."

Her hand moved over his back, her breasts pressed into his side and suddenly, an uncontrollable hunger swamped his insides. With measured movements, he pulled her out of Amira's suite and closed the door behind him.

Her hand still in his, Nikhat looked up at him. And he studied her greedily.

Her long lashes cast shadows on her cheekbones. The little light from the wall lamps bathed her mouth in golden light. And sinking under the quagmire of grief, he took the only way out.

He pushed her against the wall and took her mouth. She tasted like honey, and it went straight to all the broken places inside him, all the places that hurt for what he had done, all the places he was killing to survive another day.

He pushed his tongue into her mouth, pressed his lower body into hers until she felt his arousal, until the imprint of her soft body was all over his.

Her hands stole under his T-shirt. Her palms were against his body and, breathing hard, he pulled back. Need pinged inside him, a sharp slice of awareness running through his blood, jolting him awake as nothing had for six years.

Her eyes were hazy with desire, her mouth swollen with his kisses. He wanted to take her right there, he wanted to forget. For one blessed moment, he wanted escape. And he would find it in her body, he knew it in his bones.

The attraction between them had only intensified with time, because now she was truly magnificent, both in mind and body.

He took a step back. "Leave, Nikhat, before I——"

She slapped her hand on his mouth, shaking her head. Her eyes were bright, the pulse at her neck throbbing, as if calling for his touch. A smile danced on her lips, of understanding, of comfort. "Please don't say another word."

With shadows covering half her face and revealing the other half, she was temptation and retribution come together. This woman and his desire for her, it seemed, were very much still an uncontrollable aspect of his life. And it robbed the sweet taste of her from his mouth.

She would save him and she would damn him.

"How far will you go to alleviate the guilt?"

She flinched. And yet he couldn't stop. He didn't want to hurt her. He just wanted her to stop acting as if she cared.

"I have not been just to you. Everything I did, everything I caused, they were my actions, *Nikhat*. I could fall lower and hold you responsible, but the fact is that I did it all. I don't want your guilt or your reparation."

"Wait," she said, halting him with her fingers on his wrist. There was a resolve to her mouth that he remembered so well. "Maybe some of it is guilt, maybe some of it is a misplaced sense of responsibility.

"But whatever the past, Azeez, we're in this together

now. Whether you believe it or not, whether you want it
or not, you have my loyalty above everyone else, and you
have my friendship."

Nikhat rubbed her eyes, jolting awake as the helicopter
landed. From her seat, all she could see was a specter of
light behind her, illuminating the vast dunes of sand in
front of her. In the twilight, the dunes looked like a sea of
glistening reddish-gold, stark and yet beautiful.

She turned in place, taking in the beautiful landscape,
and stilled. A resort stood about half a mile ahead of them,
a fluorescent white glow lighting it up like a mythical for-
tress against the darkening sky. She thought she knew everything about the royal family. But she hadn't even heard
a whisper that this place existed, and she wondered if the
outside world had, either.

Thankful to Azeez for reminding her to wear a jacket,
she extracted a scarf from her handbag. She stood to the
side as he had a word with the pilot and then the chopper
left.

Only then did she make out the dark shape of a four-by-
four with the old bodyguard that she remembered, Khaleef,
at the wheel.

She wrapped the scarf snug around her face just as
Azeez motioned for them to walk toward the resort. A
gasp fell from her lips as lights came on in front of them,
illuminating a wooden bridge that resembled an old draw-
bridge from ancient times.

Laughing, she ran a couple of steps and stepped onto
the bridge. Small lights placed along either side turned on,
causing tall shadows to fall from the date trees. With tur-
reted domes and shadowed arches in front of her, she felt
as if she had stepped into the pages of a book she had read
when she was a child.

And the prince…

She turned around to find Azeez standing still at the first step, his coal-black gaze resting on her. She let the magical quality of the dusky evening seep into her.

Deciding that she wanted to help Azeez, not because her own future was dependent on it, not because her guilt demanded it, but because it would give her satisfaction, but because she cared what happened to him, was a relief. She felt as if a weight had lifted from her heart.

She was not going to weave impossible dreams, neither was she going to lie that they didn't mean anything to each other.

"A bridge, really?" she said, holding on to the humor she had found in it just seconds ago.

She glanced at the fortlike structure, the exquisitely maintained lawn in front of it with a fountain and the strategically placed lights.

"No one knows this place exists, do they?"

Resuming his slow tread, he shook her head. "Only us and a handful of servants."

"And I'm not allowed to tell anyone that I have seen it."

He reached her, and again she felt his gaze like a physical caress on her features. "No one will believe you." Said with a simple smile.

She extended her arm and he looped it around his without comment. Drawing in a deep breath, they walked ahead. Every now and then, she felt him studying her. She slowed her stride to match his, the tang of sandalwood and his skin combined, brushing up against her senses every time their bodies grazed ever so lightly.

"Going away on a trip with me to an unknown destination without Ayaan's protection or the buffer that the palace offers doesn't bother you?"

"No."

"And if I leave you here and disappear, as my brother fears?"

"I know you're hurting, and you can't see past your grief and guilt, but I know you, Azeez, probably better than anyone else. You won't leave until Ayaan himself permits you to go."

He didn't jeer, or call it misplaced confidence. His fingers tightened over her arm and Nikhat returned the pressure.

Had they finally achieved some kind of peace with each other?

She was more than reluctant to go inside as they reached the walkway that led to the foyer of the palace, when an echo of laughter and conversation reached her.

The high voices sounded familiar and yet...

Tensing, she clasped Azeez's hand and moved to stand behind him. "I thought we were supposed to be the only ones here."

Tugging at the hand that she had laid around him, Azeez met her gaze. "Go in." He ran a finger over her cheek. He inclined his head toward the palace. "Everything you require should be inside."

Suddenly, she didn't want to bid him goodbye just yet. "I would like to come with you. Wherever you're going, I'm sure I can be of help."

He shook his head, a small smile digging grooves in his cheeks. She locked her hands at her sides when all she wanted was to trace those grooves.

Was it so wrong if she did? The attraction between them was as strong as it had ever been. Why deny them both what they wanted?

"Nikhat?"

Heat suffusing her skin, she met his gaze.

"I need to be stealthy. And you, with your big eyes and

your modern attitudes, you will be hard to blend in. I will
return in two days. In the meantime, enjoy your stay."

Nikhat nodded as he left. Before she could utter another
word, she heard her name behind her. Stunned, she turned
and saw a woman of around twenty run down the stairs.
Her heart crawled into her throat, her chest felt hollow,
her head dizzy as the woman's long legs ate up the stairs.

Before she could draw another breath, Nikhat was enveloped in two pairs of arms, laughter and surprise rolling around her. Grabbing Noor and Noozat, her youngest
sisters, she looked up and saw Naima, who was four years
younger than her and closest to her in temperament.

Joy and excitement and shock and gratitude—everything
barreled through her, robbing her of speech.

Tears fell onto her cheeks and Naima's gaze met hers,
shining with her own. Nodding and sometimes replying
with a yes or no, Nikhat hugged her sisters, her heart incredibly tight in her chest.

Between Noor's questions about her return, and Naima's silent speculation, Nikhat turned around, hungry for
a glance of Azeez. But he was already gone from the bridge
and then she heard the squeal of tires. Wiping at her cheeks,
Nikhat followed her sisters inside, her heart bursting to
full with gratitude and something more that terrified the
life out of her.

She wanted to crumple to the floor and howl. Because
she was being tested again.

A rush of self-pity drenched her and for once she had
no strength to fight it with. She didn't want any reminders
of his kindness, she didn't want to remember how mag-
nificently glorious it felt when his gaze was on her, of how
effortlessly he could reduce her whole world to himself.

She had already begun to see flashes of the man he had

once been and she couldn't fight her attraction anymore. He was magnificent, he was kind and he was honorable.

How many times was she supposed to walk away without taking anything she wanted? How many times would she have to break her own heart into tiny little pieces?

She had trained herself to find satisfaction in her work and she did. She pushed herself every day to strive harder and to set new goals. She had made a life for herself. And yet, being in Dahaar brought out a loneliness she was too exhausted to see in New York. It settled deep into her bones.

And it was because of him.

She knew that. Despite every assurance she threw at herself that this time she was prepared, that she had walked away once, she still felt herself wavering, weakening and wishing for things that never could be.

CHAPTER EIGHT

REFUSING THE INVITATION to stay another night, Azeez turned just as one of his contacts stepped into the perimeter of the encampment and nodded at him.

He had visited two different camps in the last twenty-four hours across a hundred miles, trying to locate him. Glad that Nikhat wouldn't be lonely and wondering about him, because she would had her sisters not been there, he took his leave from the chief of the Mijab.

The older man clasped both his hands, his gaze dancing with a million questions.

"You'll always have a place with us," he said in an older dialect of Arabic that the bedouins had used and that his father had insisted he learn. The chief had recognized Azeez within a week of finding him in the desert, and he would always be grateful to the older man for keeping his secret.

Azeez shook his head, knowing that now he couldn't bear to live in the desert anymore. He thanked the chief for his hospitality for the past day and joined his contact.

His heart thumped loudly in his chest as he walked a mile off the beaten path where another man, a native of Zuran was waiting for him. Fierce satisfaction fueled him. The network of contacts he had built over the years was still intact, and something almost like a thrill chased his blood.

But this time it wasn't just the fiercely alive feeling that had kept him going for six years. This time it was coupled with the fact that he could go back to Ayaan and give him some much-needed information.

Signaling his contact to stay behind, Azeez slowly made his way to the small group gathered outside a tent. One man stood up from the group and walked inside as soon as he spied him. Checking that the pistol he had strapped to his left leg was still intact, Azeez stepped inside the tent.

Shock waves pulsed through him as the man turned around, and the feeble light from the two hanging lanterns illuminated his features in a garish yellow glow.

His own features wreathed in mirroring shock, Zayed Al Salaam, his oldest friend, stared back at him. "*Inshallah,* it *is* you."

Dressed in combat uniform, his face half covered in sand and mud, his dark golden eyes gleaming in the half light, Zayed covered the distance between them in two steps and embraced Azeez hard. "Of all the things to crawl out from under the desert sand...*Azeez Al Sharif...*" Zayed said, his voice harsh and yet unable to hide the tremor within. A spark of anger colored his gaze as Zayed studied Azeez with undisguised intensity. "I would have given anything to have the aid of an old friend these past years, Azeez."

Azeez closed his eyes as a cold sweat seized his insides. His breath fisted in his throat, cutting off his words.

Would there be no end to the faces that greeted him from the past? Would he never be rid of the unrelenting guilt?

He had done everything he could to bring Zayed and his sister, Amira, together, and done it so covertly that even his parents and Ayaan hadn't known. He had made it look like a treaty agreement to Zayed's uncle, Sheikh Asad, who had used Zuran and its people as pawns in his pursuit of power. Azeez had convinced his parents that marrying Zayed, the army commander of Zuran, was better for Amira than marrying Sheikh Asad's spoiled, degenerate son.

Just because Amira had begged him to help, just because, flouting every convention, his rebellious sister had fallen in love with Zayed. And Zayed with her.

And yet, he had killed her two months before her wedding to Zayed.

Had he, in a way, killed Zayed too?

"There was nothing I could do for anyone, Zayed. I was—"

Zayed shook his head. "I do not believe that. I do not believe that Azeez Al Sharif could become so heartless that he didn't even have a word for his oldest friend who had lost the woman he loved, that he had to hide himself from the world.

"I heard rumors about a man who collected information for Dahaar," Zayed spoke again, more than a hint of distrust creeping into his words now, "about a man who appeared with the Mijab suddenly six years ago...but then I thought why would a man born to rule his country hide like a coward in the shadows? Why would he forsake his parents, his friends and everyone else who needed him?"

"Zayed, you have no idea—"

"I do not, Azeez. But that is the way you wanted it, isn't it?"

The hardness in Zayed's eyes, the savagery in the tightness of his mouth, the undiluted arrogance in his words pierced through Azeez. And suddenly, he realized how much Zayed must have suffered losing Amira in such a way; Zayed, who had been captivated by her boldness and laughter; Zayed, who had never known any love or kindness.

Hardening his heart, Azeez infused steel into his voice. He was not here to reminisce with an old friend. "This from a man who pretends ignorance while his uncle wreaks havoc on the nation that he's pledged to protect, the man who should have been the rightful ruler of Zuran?"

"Not anymore, Azeez. How fortunate that I won't let an old friend return empty-handed." A dark smile crept into Zayed's eyes, any hint of the kindhearted man Azeez had known gone long ago. "Tell your Crown Prince or whoever you serve that Zuran is done being Dahaar's puppet.

"You're speaking to the new high sheikh of Zuran."

Renewed shock pulsed through Azeez. "Your uncle…"

"Has been killed by my men." A chill climbed up Azeez's spine. It was like looking at a reflection of what he had been a few months ago. And he didn't like it.

"Weren't you the one who always talked about our debt to our land, Azeez? Personal loss might have dimmed your sense of duty, whereas I have found mine only after it."

Without waiting for Azeez's response, Zayed walked out of the tent.

After waiting for a few minutes, Azeez walked out, too. Whatever the politics between Dahaar and Zuran, Zayed would never betray him.

But having seen his friend, having heard the threat in his words, Azeez was filled with renewed purpose.

There had been a coup in Zuran, which meant every small tidbit of information he could gather would be precious to Ayaan.

The chain of his guilt relenting, Azeez walked back to where his contact was waiting. He gave instructions to the man. He would need another couple of days in the desert.

He shivered as the chilly wind howled through him. The horizon stretched ahead of him in endless golden sand dunes.

He had loved the unforgiving heat, the harsh, stark landscape of the desert for as long as he could remember.

Even after he had recovered and realized he couldn't go back to Dahaar, the desert had soothed him, provided an escape from the constant guilt and shame inside him, the harsh life of traveling with the Mijab forcing him to focus on mere survival.

His mistakes, his guilt, his yearning to be close to his family, they had all been minimized. *He* had been minimized by the brutality of desert life. That's why he had clung to it for so long, that's how he had gone on living.

Could he accept never coming back here again? Could he wrench away a part of him and leave it in Dahaar when it was time to leave?

For the first time since Ayaan had captured him and dragged him to the palace against his will, the answer to his own questions wasn't absolute.

Neither could he dismiss the woman who had, just by her sheer dogged determination, breathed new will into his life.

Walking around the pool that was built in the shape of a drop of water pulled along in every direction, a gleaming blue between a maze of tall trees and walkways, Nikhat smiled, remembering every last word her sisters and she had said to each other over the past three days.

As the sun had set, small lights along the perimeter of the pool had come on, making the entire courtyard look like a jeweled necklace. The view of it from the terrace was magnificent, as if a slice of paradise had been brought to life in the middle of the desert. The contrast against the starkness of the desert dunes was lush, wondrous.

They had talked and talked until they had all been exhausted. They had laughed, cried, spent both nights, well into dawn, sitting by the pool, talking about their mother, father and so many things about the future, both near and afar.

Like Naima's upcoming wedding that Nikhat was going to miss, to Noozat's aspirations to be a midwife.

And Noor's relentless questions about the desert hideaway they had been brought to under a cloud of silence, and her awe that the royal family had done such a personal favor for Nikhat.

She had cried when it had been time to go this morning, as Noozat had railed against the situation that kept Nikhat away, while Naima had watched it all silently.

Their innocence about the world, the contentment she had seen in their eyes for their lives, fueled her own resentment in a way she had never expected, filling her with a restless energy.

She had never been like that, innocent or carefree or just plain happy.

She had always worried about her mother's health, worried about her sisters, worried about what trouble Amira would get into, worried about whether she would be allowed to pursue her dream and for how long. Despite her growing attachment to Azeez and the shock of his love for her, through it all, she had worried what the future would hold for her.

But in the end, her worrying, her cautious nature, had never helped her.

Until Richard had pursued her relentlessly for three years, she had let herself consider happiness again. She had revealed her condition, believed him when he said that he would be happy only with her. And yet, for all her worrying, his rejection had come, because suddenly he had realized he did want children, and she had been heartbroken.

Wasn't that what she had been doing since she had returned, too?

Worrying about her clinic, worrying about her sisters,

worrying about the pulse of attraction between her and
Azeez...

For the first time in her life, she didn't want to think of
the future, or the consequences of the decisions she made
today. She didn't want to be the responsible one. She wanted
to be selfish, she wanted to be carefree.

She wanted to live in the moment. She was in the most
beautiful place she had ever seen with the one man who
had always ensnared her senses with one look, one touch.

And still did.

Her fingers fluttering, she ran them over her mouth, remembering his kiss, remembering the pleasure she found
in her own body, the power that had flown through her
when he had shuddered.

The palm trees swayed stiffly in the breeze. Dusk
painted the horizon orange, casting a reddish-golden glow
over everything around her. And suddenly the evening was
awash with possibilities, as though for this night, she could
be anything she wanted.

She had wanted to be worthy of Azeez Al Sharif, the
magnificent Prince of Dahaar. And she had accepted that
she never would be.

But tonight, she would be everything that *she* wanted
to be.

A few hours later, Nikhat waited in the moonlit courtyard,
standing out among the lit-up walkways.

Lamb curry and pilaf, date cakes and sherbet made of the
finest grapes—a feast fit for a prince—had been prepared
at her command. She didn't care what the servants inside
that bustling kitchen thought of her. Only focused on the
little tidbit that she and her sisters were the only outsiders
to have ever stepped foot in here.

Her heavy hair hung loose around her face, her lips

painted pink, her eyes lined with kohl. And she was dressed in a caftan made of the brightest red, made of the sheerest silk, that she had begged Naima to lend her. A cashmere shawl lay around her shoulders to shield her from the cold.

She couldn't believe her own daring in inviting the prince to dinner so boldly. But she was past caring about her reputation, past suffering through punishments without actually committing the deed.

She refused to even indulge the prospect that he was somewhere laughing that she dared summon him.

She had waited maybe ten or fifteen minutes, when her skin prickled with awareness, when it felt as if even the air around her had come to a standstill.

Leaning against a pillar at the arched entrance, Azeez was watching her. Dressed in those same loose white pants and a white tunic, he looked like a dark shadow come to life, the expression in his coal-black eyes just as inscrutable.

He scanned her slowly from her feet in cream-colored sandals, upward to where she had cinched the caftan just below her breasts with a wide, jeweled belt, to the V-shaped neckline, threaded with intricate threadwork that was just a little shy of daring, to her mouth, her nose, her eyes and then her hair. Everywhere his gaze moved, she felt touched, she felt branded, she felt possessed.

Black fire blazed into life in those eyes that didn't miss anything. He took a step toward her, to touching distance. "You look different." Another devouring, lingering glance. "You dressed up." He cast a look behind her and took in the elaborate lengths she had gone to. "Are you celebrating something?"

"Thank you for bringing my sisters here. I…"

"I understand perfectly." He smiled, a flash of raw emotion tingeing it. He looked different, as if there was simmering energy inside him. It lit a fire along her nerves, every cell in her wanting more. "Thank you for being here, Nikhat, today and three days ago and these past weeks. I don't begrudge you your success or your happiness or whatever it is that you desire."

"You mean that."

He laughed at the obvious doubt in her tone. "I do."

His smile bared his teeth, lit up his face, and the beauty of it stole her breath. His eyes, his mouth, they had been made for laughter. And seeing him like that, it was easy to believe his goodwill. "Was your little jaunt into the desert successful then?"

"Yes." A fire erupted in his eyes. With that single word, for the first time since she had come back, she believed that the true Azeez was coming back.

She covered the little distance that separated them. Their bodies grazed, their knees bumped and a tightness rendered his features stark. And she recognized the tension in his face for what it was, reveled in the spiral of hunger that ignited in her muscles.

Giving in, she touched him.

It was the lightest of contacts—the pad of her thumb rubbing against his cheek, the heat of his body a beckoning caress. The stubble scraped her palm, the scent of his skin and soap combined tugging at her senses.

His hand moved around her nape, and with sure but infinitesimal strength, he pressed. And every particle of her being gathered behind that small patch of her skin. "You're playing with fire, Nikhat." His hand moved to her hip, his fingers branding her skin through the silk. Another thread of her control unraveled.

"I can't stop, Azeez."

His palm landed square below her chest, and her heart began a race. "Do not test the breadth of my goodwill, *habeeba.* I worked very hard to achieve it. If you tempt me today, if you tease me today, I won't walk away."

She smiled and, anchoring herself against his arms, pushed herself into his touch. The sharp hiss of his breath felt like music to her ears. "Then don't. Make love to me, Azeez."

His jaw tightened like carved stone even as a dark fire glittered in his eyes. He was more than tempted and it fueled her own desire and satisfaction. "I think seeing your sisters has twisted your mind."

She clasped his jaw with her hands. "On the contrary, visiting with them only helped me see clearly. I want this. I have always wanted this. Only, eight years ago, I never understood this fire between us."

His mouth took on a bitter slant as he tugged her hands away from her. "Is this gratitude for ordering your father to send your sisters? Because I would have done the same for any loyal servant of the palace. A simple thanks is enough for that."

Hearing him put it in that stark way, it still didn't douse the fire in her. He was creating distance between them, letting her down in the only way he knew.

But he had no idea how much she had deprived herself of, how bereft her life had been of this compelling awareness she found near him. "You're the man I've always wanted beyond reason and sense. What Richard and I had—"

He cursed so colorfully that Nikhat forgot what she was saying for a minute. "Don't manipulate me, Nikhat. I don't want to hear his name."

"Our relationship was based on mutual respect and suitability. What I feel near you, I've never felt like that, ever."

"Why now, when you threw everything I offered you before at my face and went off to pursue your dreams?"

Leaning into his body, she bent her forehead to his shoulder, the truth dancing on her lips. How could she tell him that she had never stopped wanting him? That it had never been the case of not wanting him enough. "This is not me trying to revert or start something new. This is me living in the moment."

Before her courage deserted her, before she remembered the thousand reasons this was unwise, she pulled his arm around her waist and did what she had been dying to do since she saw him, did what she had dreamed of a million times and more.

She leaned into him, until her breasts were crushed against his chest, until his groin cradled hers. Until she felt the evidence of his arousal—hard against the V of her own legs.

Air left her lungs on a long whoosh, her muscles liquefying with uncontrollable shaking. The shudder that went through him goaded her beyond reason. She pressed her mouth to his jaw, the stubble on his jaw rasping her lips in the most delicious way. "Tonight, you're not the prince who's bent upon walking away from the very thing you were born for, and I…I'm not the woman who walked away from you. For one night, will you not grant us both what we want, Azeez?"

Her pulse ringing like an incessant bell in every inch of her body, Nikhat slipped away from him and left the courtyard.

CHAPTER NINE

ONE NIGHT, AZEEZ.

Azeez stood outside Nikhat's suite, her words ringing in an endless loop in his head, traveling through his blood, moving inside him with the force of a lightning bolt.

Her proposal coming on the heels of the high he had found in uncovering information, in realizing that there was still a salvageable part of him, that he could still be of some use to his brother and Dahaar, was temptation he couldn't deny.

Standing there with her kohl-rimmed eyes staring at him with the brazen need dancing in her eyes made him feel fiercely alive, made him want to ride the wave, accept the escape she offered.

For one night, she would be his.

He pushed the door and stepped in, his gaze hungrily searching for her. She lay on the bed, her face bathed in a golden light from the bed lamp. The sheets rustled as he ventured farther in, and she rose to her knees in the middle of the vast bed, her gaze glittering with a bright hunger.

Lust and something else hit him hard in the gut, little shivers sprouting everywhere, causing tremors in his muscles.

A dazzling smile, edged with anticipation, thrill and even a flash of trepidation curved her mouth. "You came."

He felt his mouth twist into a bitter curve. "Did you doubt it?"

Her eyes closed for a second, as if she wanted to shield something from him. And he realized that she was as conflicted about this as he was, just in a different way. She had asked for this night with that characteristic bluntness that he had begun to see, but it didn't mean she wasn't nervous about it.

"You're trembling, Nikhat."

"I imagined this moment for so many years and in so many ways, Azeez, that the reality of it now, it's a little frightening."

She wore a cream-colored sleeveless nightgown that almost blended with her skin, making him think she was naked for an aching instant.

Blood rushed out of his head, leaving him with a dizzying desire. But this time, that rush wasn't followed by that clawing void. This time, she didn't disappear, this time he wasn't left with cold sheets and empty arousal. This time he wouldn't feel the shame that he felt when he looked down at the wrong face.

He came to a stop at the bed. "After those months in Monaco, my father ordered me home. For the first time in my life, I was ashamed of myself, I couldn't meet his eyes.

"I haven't touched another woman since, Nikhat. And I have been given a clean bill of health by the doctors."

He touched her chin, and tilted it up, his hand shaking. He felt her tremble, but the resolve didn't falter in her eyes.

"I'm in good health, too," she said with a small smile. "And I'm protected by the drugs I take, so…"

She placed her hands on his chest and moved them restlessly, the irises of her eyes bright like flames. She unbuttoned his shirt and pushed the edges apart. Her hands found his bare skin and he hissed out a sharp breath. Her fingers explored his chest with wanton thoroughness, curled into his chest hair, pressed into his abdomen, traced the seam of his low-slung pajamas.

Back and forth, dipping into the band now and then, until every nerve in his body was tuned into the movement of her fingers. Every muscle in him curled with anticipation.

She bent and kissed his chest, and a moan rumbled out of him. His fingers sank into her heavy tresses, the hold on his control wavering at her soft, feathery kisses. Her lips moved over his neck, his pulse, trailing wet heat all over his skin, setting a fire in its wake. The second he felt the stroke of her tongue at his nipple, he tugged at her.

She looked up, a wicked smile on her mouth, her fingers clutching his waist. Her beautiful, kohl-lined, brown eyes shimmered with desire and glittered with a raw hunger. He tightened his fingers in her hair, waited for a flash of doubt or something that would puncture the spiraling need between them.

Their hoarse little breaths whispered in the room.

Still holding his gaze, her own hazy with desire, she sank her teeth over his nipple and sucked it into her mouth.

The wet rasp of her tongue, the drag of her teeth, her soft curves rubbing up against his lower belly, right above his erection…Azeez lost the battle over his already frayed control.

He pushed her back on the bed.

Settling on his good hip, he ran his fingers over her cheek, over the pulse fluttering at her neck, to the neckline of her nightgown. Her skin was like raw silk, a sheen of pink dusting all over. The soft rise and fall of her lush breasts under the satin of her gown, her breath coming in fast little whispers, goaded him. He pressed his mouth to her neck, licked her skin, and her hands sunk into his hair.

The sight of her nipples, tight and pressed against the

silk of her nightgown sent lust stabbing at him. "Take off your gown."

She raised a heated glance to him, a soft whisper falling from her lips. "Are you not going to kiss me first?"

He tugged her lower lip with his teeth, and she gasped, before grasping his shoulders with her hands and licking his lip. He pulled back, suddenly wondering if he really could be gentle with her. "Are you going to argue over every single point in this, too?"

"I just don't see why you are the one who decides what should—"

With a quick movement that surprised even himself, he sat up and ripped up the nightgown with his hands. It tore apart, leaving her magnificent breasts tipped with dark pink areolas to his gaze.

He pushed her back onto the bed with his body and sucked her nipple into his mouth.

She let out a long, deep whimper and arched into his touch, shuddering uncontrollably under him.

He rolled the tight bud with his tongue, suckled it, breathing in the scent of her skin, immersing herself in her soft curves. It was as if a fever had taken root inside him and only plunging into her, until he could forget, until he didn't think, would help. "I get to decide because I'm the Prince, Dr. Zakhari. There are certain areas where I'll never bend to your will, and a bed with both of us in it is the first one on that list."

She tasted better than the most erotic fantasy he'd ever had of her. In his darkest moments, he had wondered how she would taste, and yet not a single fantasy was close to the raw, earthy reality of her beauty.

Struggling to his knees, he rent the nightgown all the way through. The sight of her entire body, the scent of her coating the very air he breathed, the slight quake in her toned thighs, it was a moment that blurred the memory of every other woman he had ever touched to replace her.

Nikhat could feel the intensity of Azeez's gaze on every cell, every inch of her. She moved her hands instantly to cover her sex, shocked by her own audacity. Imagining him coming here, imagining his gaze on her...the fantasy had been easy.

But the reality of his heated glance stroking over her nudity, of the trembles sparking across her skin, the need knotting her nipples, her sex aching and wet even before he touched her, completely another.

He pressed a long, lingering kiss to her abdomen, and she writhed under his masterful touch, needing more, too awash in new sensations to even speak. "You thought this would be simple, didn't you, *habeebi*?" He licked a wet trail around her navel, and every muscle in her body turned liquid.

She nodded, the ease with which he read her thoughts not at all surprising her.

He pushed her wrists out of his way. One hand moved between the valley of her breasts, locking her against the bed, while the other moved over her knees, her thighs, his breath whispering right between her legs. He flicked her knees open with the slightest touch and her thighs fell apart, her breath hitching in and out.

Her spine locked, the soft nuzzle of his nose against her thighs making it hard to pull breath into her lungs.

She was a practical woman, even with her traditional, conservative background, she hadn't been shy or prudish when she had looked at a man's naked body the first time.

But now, knowing that the most intimate part of her was open to his hungry eyes, warmth filled her inside out. A heated kiss on her thighs branded her, his jagged exhale against her skin, the pads of his fingers digging hard into her flesh, told tales of his shattering control.

And then his fingers found her core.

She threw her head back on a long moan as every inch of her came alive, a searing combination of need and desperation covering her skin. His fingers brushed against the tight bundle of nerves at her core, his strokes, long, lingering, just this short of what she needed. "Please," she said, ready to beg if need be. She pressed herself into his touch, but he wouldn't let her move the way she wanted, with the speed with which she wanted.

Every time he tugged at her nipple with his fingers, she felt an answering quiver shoot down toward her lower belly. But not enough.

Then she felt his breath on her inner thighs, felt his fingers open her to him, felt a lingering stroke of his tongue against her as if she were a feast he intended to devour. Nikhat came in a splintering shaft of light and sensation, every inch of her sex contracting and releasing, pleasure waves coiling through her lower belly.

And he still didn't stop. He didn't stop until he wrenched wave after wave of pleasure from her, until every inch of her was quaking from the unbearable intensity of her climax. Sweat dampened her skin, and the tremors slowly abated.

Pushing onto her hips took more energy than she had, but she was determined not to be a passive participant.

With her arms shaking, she clutched him and pressed a swift kiss to his mouth. She undid the strings of his pajamas, pulled them down, and the hard length of his arousal sprang into her hand.

A fresh wave of desire bolted through her. He was like velvet-sheathed steel in her hands, and she wanted that hard weight inside her, possessing her, driving into her, and more than anything, finding his pleasure in her. She ran her hands over his shoulders, his skin stretched tight over his bones, and tugged him. They fell together back on the bed. Her legs parted instantly, cradling the weight of him.

The clamoring ache began in her muscles again.

With a whispered grunt, he pushed himself up and thrust into her welcoming heat.

And Nikhat heard the long drawn-out moan that fell from her own mouth, her eyes drifting shut in exquisite pleasure.

Opening them, she found his gaze boring into hers, his breath a harsh whisper in the silence, his face a stark mask of need and desire. With a hard groan, he took her mouth again, pulled her lower lip with his teeth, ravished her until the soft tug of need became a blazing inferno in her blood again.

Digging her teeth into his shoulder, she tasted his sweat and his skin, filled herself with the scent of him. "Please, Azeez. I want more."

He entered her again, her breasts dragging against his chest, his hair-roughened legs rasping against her soft ones.

She grabbed his hips to anchor herself and he instantly winced.

"Azeez, I forgot," she whispered. He touched her forehead to his and took her mouth in a tender kiss. Something glimmered in his gaze and Nikhat was a thousand times glad that she was here with him in this moment.

Pain set his mouth into a tight line. "I cannot move like I want to, Nikhat. After the last two days in the desert, my hip…it's unbearable to move, to bear my own weight."

With a frustrated sigh, he rolled off her, and Nikhat instantly felt his loss. Turning sideways, she kissed his cheek.

She continued peppering kisses on his chest, on his throat, on his jaw. Throwing caution to the winds, she straddled him, heat tightening her cheeks.

His gaze moved over her body with a thoroughness that had her sex wet again, his mouth curved into a wicked smile. "You're a stubborn, determined woman. I forgot that."

"I want my prince and I will have him, come what may," she said, more than glad to see his smile.

A bone-deep joy flickered into life within her. Another man, she knew, would have found shame in his inability in that moment, lost his confidence. But he hadn't. She couldn't help wondering if he realized it, couldn't help but hope that she had a small part in it.

The joy that swept through her had a double edge to it because it also meant that the man she had loved long ago was beginning to come back, the man who had breathed and lived Dahaar, he was still alive beneath that clawing guilt and self-recrimination.

She clasped his erection and slowly lowered herself onto him. Heat flared within the walls of her sex, a delicious friction gliding deep into her skin. She straightened her spine, and his gaze moved to her breasts, color riding those sharp cheekbones. He drew his hand over her midriff to the valley between her breasts.

Moving to his elbows, he sent her a scorching glance. "Bend down, Nikhat. I want to kiss you."

When she dutifully did, he put that sinful mouth on her breast instead.

And Nikhat arched at the sinuous heat that pooled low in her belly again.

His teeth scraped her nipple and waves began building inside again.

"Move the way your body wants you to," he said, burying his face in her neck. "I'm all yours."

Giving in to her body's instinct, Nikhat moved. Their gazes held, their breath hitched as she moved faster, finding a rhythm that sent her once again to the edge. "Come for me, Nikhat."

His words were a raw command. And to match his words, he snuck his hands to where their bodies were joined.

His dark, rough fingers on the swollen bundle of nerves, it was the most erotic sight she had ever seen. Another coil of pressure gripped her and she clamped her thighs and moved over him.

And was rewarded by his deep, hoarse grunt of pleasure.

Nikhat came in a deep, swift swamp of sensations that had her crying his name out loud. His fingers on her hips controlling her movements, Azeez pushed harder and deeper, the slap of his flesh against hers pinging around them.

The sweat beading on his forehead, the dark fire in his gaze, the very starkness of his features, the way he lingered on that last thrust, the way every muscle in his body tightened and released as he climaxed, Nikhat watched him hungrily, even as her body felt as if it would come apart at the seams.

His breath was loud and harsh in the silence, his skin sweat slicked, his chest rising and falling, every muscle and sinew hard and shuddering.

That she had done this to this powerful, beautiful man, that it was her body that sent those spasms of pleasure through him, it was the most powerful, the most magnificent, moment of her life.

She collapsed onto him, and thought she saw a flash of shock in his gaze. When he pushed her hair from her forehead and kissed her temple, she smiled, for once, in an utterly glorious place.

Sweat coated her skin, her thighs still quaking with tiny tremors and still joined with him in the most intimate of ways.

And for the first time in her life, she reveled in every sensation that pierced her body, every little quake and flutter, every little tingle and ache, for the first time in a long time, she loved her body, damaged as it was.

Smiling, she kissed his warm skin and tasted his sweat.

She had never felt more like a woman.

Adjusting their bodies so that she was on her back, Azeez slowly pulled himself from under Nikhat. Her soft snores made him smile, but his curiosity, now blazing like a wildfire, refused to be distracted. He turned on the bed lamp on his side. The feeble light threw her lush breasts into focus and for a few minutes, he was lost.

She instantly turned sideways again, seeking warmth, and he stilled her with an arm around her waist.

And there it was.

The scar he had seen just as he had found glorious climax. Not that the blinding pleasure he had found in her was in any way blunted by his sudden observation. But now, the sheets cooling off around them, now that the edge of his hunger was blunted, he couldn't stop wondering.

The scar was about a half inch wide and was right above the hair that covered her sex. It looked precise, and he realized it was the result of a surgery.

Instantly, he thought of the name she had given him for her condition, wondered at the seriousness of it.

Exhaling a harsh breath, he pushed out the concern and curiosity, too. They had both known that this was about one night.

Glorious sex after six years of abstinence was frying his brain, warping his mind. Nikhat and he were tied together by a curious twist of fate but nothing else. It had to be.

She shivered and he pulled up the duvet to cover her naked body.

He lay back down on the bed, on his side again, and gathered her close. The scent of sex and her, a delicious combination, settled deep into his skin. He pressed a kiss to her forehead, and she snuggled into him. Her eyes fluttered open, drowsy and sated, her mouth curving into a satisfied smile. "Can we do it again?"

He laughed and tasted her mouth again.

Her eyes fluttered closed. "All I need is a little rest, and I will be ready for round two." She cracked her eyes open and winked at him. "Unless it's your creaky joints that aren't up to scratch, really. If so, we will—"

He sent his fingers on a search up her thighs, until they found her buttocks and gave her a little squeeze. She yelped and hid her face in his neck.

His throat clotted, and he marveled at how easily she had made him laugh at himself. And he stilled at another realization. Even the pain in his hip, his inability to move inside her as he wanted without pain shooting down his leg, hadn't derailed him the way it usually did. And, of course, he couldn't contest the fact that it was because it was her. He swallowed the bittersweet realization. "Sleep, *habeebi*."

The next morning, Nikhat woke alone in her bed. Sunlight glinted across every surface in her room, touching everything with a golden glow. Moving to her side, she dragged the pillow next to her toward her nose and took a deep breath. That dark scent of Azeez, with undertones of sex and sandalwood, instantly evoked tingles across her skin. Smiling, she lay there for a few more minutes, reliving last night.

The same sense of lightness and contentment pervaded her as she showered and dressed in a long cotton skirt adorned with beads and tiny mirrors that fell to her ankles, and a thin silk blouse in a pale yellow. Adding large dangly earrings that she had bought in a quirky jewelry store in Brooklyn, she studied her reflection in the mirror.

Color filled her cheeks and there was a light in her eyes. She looked every inch like a woman who had been loved, very thoroughly, last night. Refusing to let her thoughts veer into negative territory, she pulled a comb through her long hair, pulled it to fall in an angled ponytail over her shoulder and set off in search of Azeez.

The vast marble corridors of the resort, the grand archways that filled every inch of it with light, the world itself, looked like a brighter place today.

She found Azeez sitting at a table filled with breakfast dishes in a veranda off the main lounge. As it was only nine in the morning, the heat was still bearable. Pausing to catch her breath, she leaned against a wall.

His head thrown back over his chair, his eyes closed, his face was covered in sunlight. Long eyelashes cast shadows onto his gaunt cheekbones, his prominent, crooked nose shading the other side of his face from view, and his mouth…

Honeyed heat gathered in her muscles at the thought of all the things that mouth had done to her. She clutched her legs together as if she could soothe the pulsing ache at the center of her sex, desperate to stave off the yearning before it turned into something else.

She had wanted one night and she had taken it. If she continued to play with fire, she would only get burned.

"You are welcome to join me, Nikhat." The hint of teasing in his tone had relief sweeping through her. She exhaled deeply, and smiled, more than glad that he was in that wicked, humorous mood. It was only a fragile cover over the deep passion underneath, the heated intensity of his emotions, but she welcomed it anyway. "I won't bite. Not now and not here."

Simple, mocking words. Yet it felt as if he had caressed her with his fingers. She sat down on the opposite chair and met his gaze.

It swept over her slowly, as if he had been waiting to do just that. "You look very—" he inclined his head, still looking, still devouring, and her heart thudded "—carefree today. Very much…"

She raised a brow, loving the wicked gleam in his eyes. "Very much like a satisfied woman? I did score—" she scrunched her face into a mock frown "—four times."

He erupted into rich laughter, and it was impossible not to join him.

Shaking his head, his mouth still curved into a wide smile that dug grooves on his stubbled cheeks, he leaned forward. "I was going to say reckless."

"Remember that time when you came back from university and wouldn't stop strutting around the palace, as though you were lord of everything you surveyed, and Ayaan and Amira bugged you incessantly—"

"I *was* the lord of everything I surveyed."

Her breath hitched in her throat. The sheer, undiluted arrogance in his words, it was so much like the old him. "Fine. Like a…." She clicked her fingers. "You were like a peacock strutting your feathers or your *mighty sword* in this case," she snorted in mock disgust. "It was so easy to see through you."

Slashes of deep color marked his cheekbones. "Your vocabulary, I see, has become just as enriched as the rest of you, *habeebi*." His eyes wide, he ran his fingers over his eyebrows, his mouth still wreathed in smiles. "Of all the things to remember, Nikhat? I never told them. At least, Ayaan, not until a couple of years later. I can't believe you…"

Now it was her turn to blush under the dawn of a slow

intensity in his gaze. "My obsession with you had already begun. I was years ahead of everyone else in biology. God, my fourteen-year-old self burned with jealousy. And I knew exactly what put that smug, self-satisfied smile on your face." She pointed her finger toward her face, unable to stop smiling.

"I believe that's what you see today."

Shaking his head, Azeez studied her, wondered at how easy she made it to laugh, how she reminded him of everything that had been good about the past.

Because there *had* been good things in the past.

He could finally see the brilliance of Ayaan's idea.

Nikhat, with her joyful stories about their family, with her infallible strength and loyalty, was the perfect medicine that his brother could have brought for Azeez.

And it was working.

Here he was, just weeks later. He had made love to a woman, the fact that it was she—he chalked it up to the curious quirk of fate—he had found invaluable information for Dahaar, he was laughing.

It would be so easy to get used to this. To having her in his bed, to laugh with her out of it. Already, she was insinuating herself into his life again, already the urge to share his shame with her, to find that relief, too, it was overwhelming.

She had him wonder if he wanted more from life, made him wonder about the future. And she made him want to forget and move ahead. And that hope, he did not deserve it.

He couldn't let her be anything more than a temporary drug on the road to recovery, couldn't let her distract him from his true purpose. He couldn't let her believe that this had been anything more than a brief interlude. He would help Ayaan and then he would leave.

Suddenly, he couldn't wait to be his brother's prisoner again.

She blinked as he stood up. A stillness emerged in her body, her laughter inching into something else as he moved closer.

He silenced the clamor of regrets inside.

It was better this way. He had nothing to offer her.

His fingers moved over her mouth as he settled on the table in front of her. Frantic for another taste of her, he took her in a devouring kiss that had their lips clinging, sucking, drawing breath from each other in seconds. She clasped his cheek as he trailed his mouth over her temple.

"Ayaan has got this whole science of managing me down very well, it seems. You were exactly what I needed. I have been thinking of myself as a cripple, have let everything about me filter down to just that one fact. I will never be able to ride a horse again, or run or, apparently, make love to a woman the way I want to...But you have also made me realize everything I *can* do. Maybe have even given me a new lease on life."

He couldn't hold back the warmth in his words. It was her due.

He pushed a tendril of her hair back. "Last night will be as memorable to me as it is to you, Nikhat.

"Now, it is time we returned. I have some time-sensitive information for Ayaan. And I am sure you can't wait to get back to being the stern doctor who has to get the dissolute, arrogant prince in shape so that he's off your plate and your life can get back on track."

CHAPTER TEN

PRINCESS ZOHRA REQUESTS your presence at dinner tonight in the Royal Hall.

The palace maid's softly spoken instruction ringing in her head, Nikhat followed her down a corridor she had never visited before. The maid, after showing her to huge double doors, partially open, left. Pushing one door ajar, Nikhat stepped in.

And her jaw met her chest at the sight that greeted her.

Every surface she saw was either golden or silver, including the edges of the huge rectangular table. Intricately wrought silver-and-gold knives and forks and plates glinted in the light thrown from the crystal chandelier overhead. The crystal had a gold tint to it, casting a bright yellow glow on everything in the room.

There were portraits of generations of Al Sharifs on the walls. Vases were overflowing with exotic flowers. Velvet-cushioned heavy chairs sat around the table, the back of each intricately carved with the Dahaaran insignia of a sword.

And on the table, an unending array of mouthwatering dishes beckoned.

Azeez stood in the darkened corner of the room, and yet she felt his gaze on her, as though he had touched her.

"Hello, Nikhat."

Running a hand over her midriff, Nikhat nodded. She couldn't speak, couldn't move, pinned to the spot by the energy instantly crackling in the air around them.

They hadn't seen each other since they had returned from the desert four days ago. She had no idea who was avoiding whom, or maybe they both were.

She had thought she would take the plunge and taste paradise for one night. What she hadn't realized was how hard it would be to have tasted it once and then having to live with the fact that it would never be hers again. A fierce need to leave a mark on him, that's what she had wanted. Instead, she felt as if she was the one who had walked away scarred, again.

She startled and turned as she heard Princess Zohra behind her. Greeting her with a nod, she walked back toward the entrance, realizing the significance of the occasion. Of course, the princess would want to celebrate.

Holding the wave of emotion threatening to pull her under, Nikhat was about to leave when the princess stopped her. "I had the servants invite you on purpose, Nikhat. My family is not with me and you have—" she flicked a knowing look toward Azeez, and Nikhat could only be thankful he didn't notice "—brought peace of mind to me in more than one way."

Her stomach twisting, Nikhat wet her lips. "I do not belong at this dinner."

Before Nikhat could leave, Ayaan entered the hall.

Unable to excuse herself, Nikhat took the seat next to Azeez. His gaze took in her shaking hands, and she clasped them rigidly in her lap, wishing herself anywhere but here.

"You're shaking. Are you in pain again?"

She shook her head. Ayaan dismissed everyone else, even the waiting servants. His hands on her chair, he leaned down and took Princess Zohra's mouth in a kiss that sent heat rushing to Nikhat's cheeks.

Next to her, Azeez leaned back into his seat, stretching his right leg. "Do you wish us to leave, Ayaan?" There was more than a hint of teasing in his voice and Nikhat instinctively turned.

He was grinning, and the joy in his face momentarily wiped everything else from her mind.

Leaning over the chair, his arm still around Princess Zohra's, Ayaan smiled at Azeez. "We are celebrating and… we would like you to be part of it. Zohra had an ultrasound scan today." He nodded at Nikhat. "We're having twin boys."

Nikhat wanted to look away and yet she devoured every expression, every nuance in Azeez's face.

He became very still in contrast to the restless energy that poured off him; even the air around him seemed to hang in suspension. Slowly, he blinked, as though coming out of a deep fog.

His gaze caught hers for an infinitesimal second and the flash of something in it left Nikhat shaken to the core. She felt unbearably frozen inside. And she fought the feeling.

She had enough to feel guilty about, enough things that she couldn't change about herself. She didn't want the burden of his disappointment, the burden of his lost dreams.

Her hands gripped the hard wood at her sides and still, she could not look away.

Finally, when he recovered, it felt like a lifetime even if it had been nothing but a few seconds. When he looked at Ayaan, there was nothing but undiluted happiness there. "It is cause for celebration." He cleared his throat. "The future king of Dahaar is going to be born," he said with such pride, such joy, that tears rose to her eyes.

Why it should hurt so much after all these years, why it

twisted her stomach in such pure agony, Nikhat couldn't say. She had delivered babies, she saw pregnant women on a daily basis and yet, this time, she couldn't stave off the pain no matter what she did.

Azeez walked to Ayaan and clapped him on the back. "You are a prayer come true, Princess Zohra." His breath hitched on the words as he pulled the princess out of her chair and enveloped her in a fierce hug that had the princess staring at him with shock filling her beautiful eyes. "For Dahaar, for my family, but most of all, my brother. Even the doctor has to agree that this calls for a drink," he said, throwing a look at Nikhat.

Nikhat nodded, her heart in her throat, her vision full of unshed tears. She forced herself to congratulate Ayaan, forced herself to smile even as her heart shattered in her breast again.

Pain sliced through her and she gasped for breath. How could this pain be as sharp as ever? How had she found herself in this moment again?

She felt Azeez's continued scrutiny, his puzzled look at her petrified silence over the next hour, but there was nothing she could do. Every moment of the royal family's happiness sent piercing pain through her and she sat through it all, wishing herself anywhere else in the world, yet bound to him, more by her own heart than any promise she had made.

Azeez finished his drink, the dark chasm of Nikhat's heavy silence next to him grating on his nerves. She had hardly touched her food, hardly spoken a word all through dinner. They had shared one beautiful night. She was not his concern, he reminded himself.

He turned his attention to his brother. The ever-present

shadow of tiredness gleamed under Ayaan's wide smile. "You were not present during the scan?"

Ayaan shook his head and clasped Zohra's fingers with his. "No. There was an official summons requiring Father's presence in Zuran last night and I went. Thanks to you, I was at least prepared."

"Zayed?"

Ayaan nodded. "He proposed changes to the economic policy Dahaar has with Zuran. He is threatening to declare war if we don't alter the terms of the peace treaty."

"That treaty was signed almost fifteen years ago. I remember Father telling me how he had to force Sheikh Asad not to gamble away all of Zuran's oil to fill his treasury."

Ayaan looked at him with increasing interest. "Then Zayed has conveniently decided to forget it. He claims Father bullied him into signing bad terms for Zuran with the threat of Dahaar's army. It's clear he views our alliance with Siyaad as a threat."

"It's just a threat to get Dahaar to—"

"I don't think you can make that claim anymore. He's not the man our sister was going to marry, Azeez. You saw him. Assure me he's not changed and I will…"

Azeez shook his head, knowing that Ayaan was right. The man he had seen had been but a shadow of his old friend. And suddenly, for the first time since he had been shot, Azeez realized what a gift he had in his family, in Nikhat.

Zayed was, and had always been, truly alone in the world.

"I will not call Father back for this. Not after everything he's shouldered alone for all these years. I need help, Azeez."

"You have experienced staff for—"

"You have a bloody doctorate in trade policy and economics. Father prepared us to complement each other, Azeez. For you to rule and for me to aid you. If you're determined to leave, at least help me while you are here."

As though Ayaan had rolled a small explosive amidst the gleaming silverware on the table, the air leached out of the room. Princess Zohra's gaze clashed with Azeez's, a defiant challenge blazing in it.

Instant denial rose to his lips. He felt Nikhat shift closer to him just as he opened his mouth. Beneath the table, she clasped her fingers with his, and he wondered if she realized what she was doing.

"Fine. Have the original treaty and the amendments he is suggesting delivered to me. I will take a look." Tugging Nikhat up along with him, he forced the fury rattling inside him to a corner.

Azeez barely kept his temper under control until Ayaan and Zohra vacated the vast hall. Planting himself in Nikhat's way, he stood leaning against the closed doors.

"What kind of game are you playing now?"

She looked wary, a haunting strain around her usually placid features. "I'm not playing any game."

"Just because we—"

She flinched and reached out a hand, as if to ward off an attack. "Please, Azeez."

The poisonous words died in his throat.

Anything he would have said would have been wrong on so many levels. He didn't want to cheapen or dirty what they had shared. His life had been enough of a wasteland for him to know that despite the past and the future what they had shared was special.

And whatever this restlessness simmering under his skin, that was gaining power inside him, that was beginning to fester as painfully as the guilt, it was not her fault. She had, as always, done what was required of her.

It was him. Suddenly, everything he had been so sure of a few weeks ago felt like shifting ground, and he didn't know how to anchor himself.

He saw Nikhat swallow, struggle to speak. "I was about to remind you that you decided to do whatever you could to take the stress off Princess Zohra. It is why I am here, Your Highness."

Her address felt like a slap in the face. "Do not call me that."

She laughed and he turned to look at her. It was a low, haunting sound, so full of despair it made the hairs on his neck stand. "No? Can you hear yourself? I finally understand the audacity of hope in Ayaan's eyes.

"How long has it been since you looked at yourself in a mirror, Azeez?

"You need a blood transfusion to be anything but the Prince of Dahaar. Not a bullet wound, not your self-loathing, not the fact that you are determined to live a half-life, nothing can change the fact that you are a prince through and through.

"Dahaar—its politics, its welfare, its economics—it's the very blood that gives you life."

"Enough, Nikhat."

Instead of heeding his warning, she moved closer to him. Her gaze blazed with some unknown anguish, her hands fisted by her sides…the tightness of her shoulders, the tension in her lithe frame coiling tighter and tighter around them. And beneath all that, the heat of her body stroked the slow burn in him to a smoldering fire.

"Admit that a part of you craves it even now, admit how much it tortures you that Ayaan is taking your place, that it is Ayaan's son who will be the next king of Dahaar.

How much it galls you that Ayaan is taking everything that should have been yours?"

He flinched, the cutting fury of her words stealing into him, hurting him.

"Yes, it does. It tortures me that Ayaan suffers every night, it tortures me that my father and mother have to grieve their daughter—a daughter who was about to get married—it tortures me that wherever I turn, there's still evidence of the destruction I wrought."

She didn't back down even then. Her lush mouth settled into a stubborn set, her chin tilting defiantly. "I know how much Amira loved you. Even if you were somehow responsible, she would have forgiven you, Azeez. She would have never wanted this…half-life for you."

"But she's not here. Because of me."

"How? How is it your fault that a terrorist group attacked all three of you and killed her?"

"They didn't attack us. I lured them there with bait. I passed on information that I would be there, set up a meet. They had been issuing threats for months.

"Without my father's permission, without letting him know my dangerous plans, I planned to stay behind with a small unit and capture them. He dismissed that unit without my knowledge, and too late I realized Ayaan and Amira stayed back.

"They stayed back to talk to me. They stayed back because they were worried about me, because I had been avoiding them. And they were caught in the crossfire."

He pushed the words out through a throat raw with ache and suddenly, it felt as if the choke hold of his own guilt and recriminations relented. Just a little. He felt her tentative touch on his shoulder, and shuddered at the thought of facing her.

But when he did, he didn't see sympathy or pity. He only saw his own pain reflected there, he only saw grief.

And then it wasn't so hard to speak anymore. It was a relief to put his agony into words, to let her see all of his sins, all of his guilt.

"I saw her take a bullet, Nikhat, one that should have been for me. I saw a bullet graze my twenty-year-old brother's head. I saw them fall one after the other, I saw those bastards drag them away and I could do nothing.

"I brought destruction to them.

"And all because I had become reckless, because I hadn't cared whether I lived or died.

"She's dead because of me. My brother has nightmares to this day because of me. I let my emotions get the better of me. Because you left, I went on a reckless rampage.

"The Golden Prince, who had never wanted for anything, who had never had anything denied him, I couldn't handle your rejection. That's how emotionally strong I was. That kind of man, who can fragment so easily, that kind of man who's at the mercy of his emotions, that man is not fit to be a king.

"But Ayaan is.

"There was a point when I thought Al Sharifs, the dynasty that ruled over these lands for two centuries, would end because of what I did. Ayaan's news today…it fills me with joy, it feels like I can draw a breath for the first time. It galls me to look at him, yes, because he is a better man than I am.

"I do not care, however, whether it is he or I on the throne, whether it is my son or his that will rule Dahaar next. I'm not guilty of that sin."

Nikhat rubbed the back of her neck with her fingers, rocking on the balls of her feet, her breath coming and going in hard bursts.

"Nikhat?" He grabbed her as she swayed. "Why do you care so much about this…about whether I leave Dahaar or not?"

"I don't want to," she said. "My life will be so much simpler if you leave. And yet, I see you and…" She had paid a high price, one he hadn't asked of her, one that she suddenly wasn't so sure about, so that he could do his duty, so that he could be the man he was destined to be, so that he could father the heir to the throne. "Leaving him to deal with all this when you can help, leaving him to deal with Dahaar, with your parents when you hold yourself responsible for all this, it sounds like the opposite of penance.

"This sounds like cowardice."

"What would you have me do, Nikhat?"

The vulnerability in his words shook her, the trust in his dark gaze, how she wished she deserved it. She clutched his hands and tugged him toward her. She kissed his cheek, loving the raspy texture, holding him as if she never wanted to let go. "I think you have punished yourself enough. Your heart is your greatest gift, Azeez. But you won't listen to me, will you?" She ran her fingers over his temple, tracing the strong lines of his cheekbones, loving him a little more in that moment.

How could she not?

"Tell Ayaan what you told me. Tell him why you want to leave, Azeez, the true reason. And if you still want to be punished, then accept whatever he decides for you as your sentence."

She didn't know if her answer angered him or affected him at all. He only stared at her for what felt like a long time before he turned around and left.

Nikhat reached for the wall behind her and crumpled against it. She felt as if she would shatter into a million pieces. Or maybe she already had and this was how it felt to fall apart.

Do you think I care whether it is he or I on the throne, whether it is my son or his son that will rule Dahaar next?

It felt as if the one decision that she had built her life around had suddenly morphed, changed shape into a question rather than a statement, and the foundations of her life were fracturing around it.

Even when she had ventured toward happiness again with Richard, she had only been hurt by his sudden change of heart that he wanted children. It had made her realize that she had been right about not wanting to give Azeez the choice between her love and the throne.

But now she was caught inside a hell of her own making, hating herself, pitying herself, questioning every decision she had ever made to arrive at this point in her life.

Because, as long as she had been confident that she had done the right thing, she had borne any amount of pain, soldiered on with her life even after losing everything that had been precious to her. But if Azeez hadn't cared whether it was he or his brother who inherited the throne, or whose child was the heir...

She sank to the floor in a boneless heap, and wrapped her arms around herself.

The only thing she understood amidst all that, the one thing she knew was that she couldn't bear to see him leave, she couldn't even breathe at the thought of not seeing him again, of not feeling his rough hands on her, of not feeling his hard body shudder in her arms, of not seeing that gaze sear through her, owning her, claiming her.

She had fought tiny little battles all her life to be able to follow her own heart, to be able to make her own destiny, to have the right to do as she willed.

Now she felt all that strength unraveling. All she wanted

was to give herself over, body and will, into his hands, and forget everything.

She would always love him, she realized with a shudder. And she was desperate enough to hold on to him for as long as she could.

The next morning, Azeez paced the length of his brother's office, shocked at the difference in his own mind since he had been here only a few weeks ago.

The room still dealt a swift kick to his gut, but at least he could breathe after those first few moments, he could bear to stand inside.

His mind, however, would not let go of Nikhat's words.

Cowardice, that was it. Every action of his, every decision he had made in the last few years was full of his own cowardice, his ego, his dented pride. He had hidden it all under guilt, called it penance.

But she was right.

How could he walk away now knowing everything he did?

Maybe if Ayaan hadn't brought him back, maybe if he hadn't seen how much Ayaan needed him, maybe if he hadn't learned today that he was going to be an uncle... he felt divided in half, the unrelenting questions pounding through him.

Maybe he was not fit to rule Dahaar, but he could still be its servant, couldn't he? He could serve his brother, he could shoulder some of his burden.

Where was the honor in walking away from the wreckage he had created?

He walked to the portrait of his family, and let the tears prick behind his eyes. Maybe he was not completely broken. It had taken him years to realize what his father had always taught him.

His father, Azeez and Ayaan—they had all been born with a purpose—to serve Dahaar and its people. And for years, embroiled in in his own guilt and inadequacy, he had forgotten that. He had forgotten what he was capable of, he had forgotten what it felt like to be the man he was destined to be.

"Azeez?"

He turned around and faced Ayaan. His copper gaze curious, his brother stared at him warily. "Is everything all right?"

Nodding, Azeez pointed to the file he had left on the table. "I have taken a look at the amendments to the treaty. What Zayed's committee is suggesting is not completely disagreeable. If I were the new high sheikh of Zuran, my first act would be to restore all the rights his uncle signed away to their oil. My guess is that he needs this to happen so that he can thwart the High Council. Remember, in Zuran, the High Council has the final vote on everything, even electing the sheikh. If we back his victory now, we will have gained a powerful ally, we can use this to better tax treaties, even."

His shock apparent in his slow steps, Ayaan grabbed him in a sudden hug. A shudder racked his brother's body. "I forgot how much you used to rub my face in the fact that you're better than me at everything."

"Believe me, Ayaan, I'm not." For once, the memories that swamped him did not steal Azeez's breath. He cleared his throat. "I have also prepared an official statement for you. Run it by your economic adviser. We cannot—*Dahaar* cannot—look weak to Zayed. By agreeing to this, we are showing good faith, not capitulating under his threat of war. He needs to understand that."

His brother picked up the statement Azeez had written

by hand, his brow tied. "This is brilliant." Only then did he look at Azeez. "Were you up all night?"

"Yes."

Pulling the chair back, Ayaan crumpled into it with a harsh exhale. The strain on his brother's features intensified the thread of shame Azeez felt. "Because you are preparing to flee in the middle of the night?"

Azeez felt his temper flare but held it in check. He had deserved that. "My fate is in your hands, Ayaan."

"What do you mean?"

"I will tell you why I didn't come back, why I quake at the idea of meeting Father's eyes, why I can't bear to see Mother's tears. And then you decide. You decide my fate and I will accept it."

CHAPTER ELEVEN

AZEEZ CLOSED THE door to his bedchamber. He was exhausted from little sleep last night and after the eviscerating discussion he had had with Ayaan.

There had been no judgment, no anger, nothing but shared loss in his brother's eyes.

His brother and he had shed tears over their sister, he had seen what grief Ayaan hid under the strong facade, understood why the past haunted him in the form of his own nightmares, his worry for Zohra's health, his mounting concerns about Zohra's home country, Siyaad, and its administration until her brother Wasim came of age…

From every word he had said and every complaint he had left unsaid, it was clear that Ayaan was barely keeping up. They had both known and accepted that such was this life, that beneath the palaces and decadent lifestyles that the public saw, running a country was hard work, with peace treaties that fell apart at a minute's notice at a perceived insult, it was strategy cloaked as diplomacy, it was sometimes picking the least evil choice in a host of bigger ones.

His father had shouldered it all with their mother by his side, and Ayaan would with Princess Zohra by his side. And Azeez would aid him, he would do everything he could to share his brother's burden.

He would spend the rest of his life being his brother's servant.

Instantly, his thoughts turned to Nikhat. He had been avoiding her, even as her words hadn't left him alone. She had looked as if she would fall apart, as if somehow his grief had morphed her. He longed to hold her, kiss her, wanted to comfort her, and yet, he could not.

He wanted to tell her that he was going to stay in Dahaar, thank her for helping him find himself again, his sense of purpose again, thank her for sharing his shame and his pain…the list was endless.

But he wouldn't stop there. He knew what it was to kiss her, to hold her and to know every intimate sound she made, and he couldn't go back to not wanting that.

And to want her like that again, to let her tangle his emotions just as he was beginning to find a purpose to his life again, it was not acceptable.

He spied a rectangular yellow envelope on his desk marked Confidential and froze.

The reports he had requested four days ago while Nikhat had been sleeping in his bed had finally arrived.

He had no doubt it would have everything he had asked for—photocopies of every doctor's report that had been written about the woman who had skewered him with her questions, who was bent upon knowing every dark and cracked part of him. And a comprehensive write-up translating it into layman's words for him.

Walking past the desk to the dark wood cabinet behind it, he extracted a crystal decanter and poured himself a drink. He hadn't touched one in five weeks, not since he had thrown the bottle at her. He didn't have to now, the sane part of him whispered. He needn't have the drink, nor did he need to open that envelope and read what was inside.

He could trash it and walk away from this moment, forget he had ever requested it. He didn't have to know what she had been through. Not even she was worth playing this dangerous game of wills with his own emotions.

He put down the glass with a thud that resonated around him. Tearing open the envelope, he pulled out the sheaf of papers and proceeded to read.

Report after report of words he didn't understand, just as he had assumed. She had seen a lot of doctors, here and abroad. Finally he found the page that would make sense of the technical words.

Halfway through the succinct write-up, he froze, the very axis of his world tilting in front of his very eyes.

Nikhat might never be able to have children.

Suddenly, every word out of her mouth, every action of hers, made sense. She had left him not because she had loved her dream of being a doctor, her freedom more than she had loved him.

His chest felt tight, a hollow ringing in his ears.

What would he have done if she had told him the truth? He would have never thought any less of her, he would have...

His limbs felt restless, his skin too tight to contain the emotions within him.

She had never told him the entire truth. She had sacrificed her own happiness and his so that he could do his duty. She was every bit the magnificent woman he thought she was.

And with the realization brought threadbare hope and excruciating anguish. Anguish that she had never trusted him enough with her secret, trusted him enough with the truth.

After everything he had just told her yesterday, after the maelstrom of guilt and pain he had felt just recounting that horrible day to Ayaan again, he should have felt nothing. Being numb would have been a blessing in more ways than one.

But of course not. Apparently, he still hadn't killed everything inside him that felt, and hurt and was wounded. He wanted to reach inside him and pluck it out with his bare hands, he wanted to stop feeling so much.

And so he went to see her, the woman who, it seemed, would always have something to teach him, who would always guide him.

Nikhat shivered even though the water that gushed out of the gleaming silver-and-gold faucets was piping hot, and the steam from it curled her hair around her face. The subtle scent from the rose oil that she had poured into the water teased her nostrils, coating her skin with it.

If anyone had asked her what she had done today, she had no answer for them. She had wandered through the palace, wherever she was allowed, until an old guard had stopped her and inquired if she was okay.

Flushing, she had looked around herself, claimed that she was lost and walked back to her own suite.

The grandiose decor of her quarters, the view of the sky glimmering with stars, the sweeping arches and walkways in the courtyard below her balcony, nothing could hold her attention. Feeling as if the walls would close in on her, she had finally fled for some air.

And here she was now, waiting for the minimal staff to retire for the night, waiting for the minute when she could go to him. Maybe if she saw him, if she touched him, this chill she felt inside might abate.

Here in the palace there was still a fragile thread of sanity intact inside her, a small shred of propriety.

She scooped up a handful of water and threw it on her

face, to stifle the hysterical little laugh that threatened to escape her.

It was so pathetic—this tiny little nod to decorum, this bone-deep clinging to tradition when her entire world was crumbling under the weight of her very own confusion.

Pulling her wet hair back with one hand, she reached for a towel, when he suddenly appeared at the entrance to the bathroom.

His jet-black hair gleamed with wetness, his unshaved chin adding to the dangerous glint in his dark eyes. His collarbone stuck out from the opening of his white cotton shirt.

The sheer decadence of the marble-and-gold decor, the glitter of the mirror that caught the tiny little lights from the chandelier in the dome-shaped ceiling, the extravagantly soft cotton in her fingers—everything she had marveled over on her first night here in the palace—vanished in his presence.

Nothing could match the stark power of the man looking at her as though he owned her. Nothing could add or take away from the raw sensuality that was a very part of his nature.

He didn't say a word, his gaze traveling over her nakedness thoroughly, the fire in it burning higher and hotter. And she didn't shy from it, though her fingers tightened over the towel.

"Get out of the tub."

His words, spoken in low, raw tones did what the savage gleam in his eyes hadn't. It sent a prickle of apprehension across her skin, drawing goose bumps. Something felt wrong, something more than the fact that she had pushed him into reliving his worst nightmare because she had wanted to be sure she had made the right decision.

"I'm sorry about last night, Azeez. I never meant to push you—"

He leveled another look at her, and more words wouldn't come. A chill that had nothing to do with her nudity clamped her spine. Shivering, she took the chance to dry her skin.

The sound of the water whooshing out of the tub was gone, leaving them in heavy, sweltering silence. She dragged the towel against herself over one arm, then the other. His looming presence called to her like nothing she had ever known, and she looked up.

Molten fire blazed in his eyes. The fire of the desire between them, she understood. But this thing that was swelling and arcing between them, it was tempered with something else, something that she didn't understand.

She was already as fragile as a house of cards. One harsh breath of air and she felt as if she would come undone.

He had never refrained from telling her what he thought, never held back the force of his passion, or fury or anything.

Holding one edge of the towel over her breasts, she pressed it to her midriff, and suddenly realized he was within touching distance. A soft gasp fell from her mouth as he plucked the towel from her hand, threw it behind him. His long fingers clasped tight around her wrist, he pulled her forward until she landed against his chest, splashing his unbuttoned cotton shirt with drops of water.

Her fingers latched on to the soft fabric, her nipples tightening into needy little points. And then and only then did she realize the storm of fierce emotion that he was holding at bay with sheer will. It was in the way his fingers held her hips—pressing, possessing, branding instead of caressing, in the way he pushed the rigid length of his arousal into her belly, in the way he shivered, as if it cost him every ounce of control not to snap.

Her legs trembling under her, she gazed up at his face and an answering shudder went through her. He looked

gloriously angry, every inch of his angular face taking on
a forbidden cast.

And still, she was not afraid; still, she did not ask him
to release her as every rational instinct in her was urging
her to; still she did not try to pull herself from his grasp.
Instead, she listened to the primitive one, the one that had
roared with anger and ache that long-ago day when she
had met the doctor in New York, the one who she had
shut away behind a cage of practicality and duty with the
chains of her will.

It made her stand her ground, it made her clasp his cheek
in a brazen challenge.

He inhaled in a long-drawn breath. His thumb moved
over her cheek, her jaw, before settling on her lower lip. If
she had felt the anger simmering in his eyes, just before
his thumb pressed against her bottom lip, she didn't know.
She could only feel the little shivers spewing into life all
over her, could only feel her breasts getting heavier, a rush
of wetness gathering at her sex.

She dug her fingers into his shoulders as he continued
to trace the shape of her lip, pushed his thumb inside her
mouth. Heat bloomed low in her stomach and she sucked
his finger into her mouth.

Instinct drove her and she pressed herself into him, the
hard, pulsing weight of his erection leaving an imprint on
her belly. Shock waves pulsed between her legs and she
clutched hard with a moan.

She bent her head and licked the crook of his neck,
pulled the scent of him deeper into her lungs until all she
could feel was him. She wanted to say something, ask him
what was wrong, comfort him if she could, and yet words
would not come, as if her body was drowning under the
avalanche of sensations, as if she was finally incapable of
processing a thought, much less speaking it.

His hand around her waist, he suddenly moved and tugged her along with him. Anticipation and need burst into flames under her skin, heating her up as he positioned them in front of the huge marble vanity, facing the mirror.

The glitter from numerous gilded light fixtures above the mirror bathed them in golden light. She pulled another breath through her parched throat, and he shrugged his shirt off his shoulders.

She feasted her eyes on his chest, on the dark nipples, the hunger in her rising, her skin feverish with need. When he dropped his loose trousers and his erection grazed her buttocks, she gasped, as if she was drowning. Or maybe she was. But she didn't care. She didn't care about anything, couldn't think of anything except the thought of that rigid, velvet weight pushing inside her, filling all the empty places she had covered up.

Her breasts became heavy, her nipples turning into unbearable points of need at the luscious gleam in his eyes.

"Have you ever spoken the truth with me?"

His question shattered the silence and yet she couldn't digest the weight of it as his finger drew maddening circles around her nipple. The anticipation coiling inside her lower belly was too much to bear, as if the cognitive part of her brain was struggling to react under so much sensory input.

She let out a long, keen moan as his fingers finally pinched her nipple. Tremors arrowed down, drenching her sex in wetness. Her spine arched into him, she grasped his wrists to keep his fingers on the tight buds, needing more, ready to beg for more.

But he didn't comply and disappointment cut through her. With his hand at the base of her spine, he didn't let her arch into him. His fingers moved restlessly over her breasts, touching, not touching her nipples, moved over to her stomach, never still, never touching her where she wanted to be touched. An anguished sob rose through her the moment she realized.

He was punishing her. This, tonight, it was not about making love. This was about the fury that was bursting inside him seeking an outlet. And not because he was denying her what she wanted.

It was mastery over her mind that he craved. And he didn't leave a doubt. He didn't need to speak to say it. It was in everything he didn't say, in the way he wouldn't even meet her eyes.

And yet she couldn't deny him, yet she couldn't summon the single word *no*. Because if she did, he would stop. And she didn't want him to stop. And therein lay his victory, therein lay the prize he was after.

He pressed his palm at the base of her spine, willing her to yield. And she did.

Supporting herself on her hands, she leaned over until her breasts touched the marble. Her nipples tightened at the cold, but it was one snowflake compared to the burning flames of her desire.

She felt his mouth press into her shoulder blade, trail down, leaving wet heat. Sometimes he licked, sometimes he bit the flesh. And every stroke of his tongue, every drag of his teeth pushed her a little closer to the edge.

"Spread your legs." His tongue licked the seam of her ear shell, his voice like a silken caress.

Heat streaking her inside out, Nikhat did. His palm cupped her mound, the heel of it rubbing against the sensitive bundle of nerves within her core. She was panting now, moving her body to a rhythm only she knew, climbing higher and higher. Her forehead was clammy with sweat. His arm wrapped around her waist, he stopped her little movements.

Her release was so close, she could taste it on her tongue.

Her knuckles showed white where she gripped the marble, her entire body shuddering like a bow, ready to fall apart with one stroke.

But he didn't give her that.

He pressed his body into hers until his erection rubbed against her, and she turned her head and looked at him.

Desire. Anger. Fury. Everything danced in his ebony gaze.

"Azeez, please don't shut me out now." She choked on the words rushing out of her, struggling to say them, fighting to say them right.

But instead of answering her, instead of shouting at her, instead of flaying her with that wicked tongue of his, he gripped her hips and entered her in one long, deep thrust.

She clutched her eyes closed and whimpered as her nerves short-circuited and she orgasmed in a flurry of pleasure. His hoarse cry clashed against hers, drowning them in the sound of their mingled relief.

The waves piled and pooled over her lower belly, and she shivered. One arm over her spine, one around her waist, he held her tight against him until the little tremors subsided, until she could once again feel her body, until the receding waves washed away the profound sense of joy and fulfillment she had found.

Once again, leaving her empty.

She was laid out in front of him like a feast, and Azeez could see nothing past her trembling flesh, feel nothing past how she felt around him. He ran his hands all over her back, her skin like raw silk under his hands, her body molding to his will and his desire.

And still, he was not satisfied. Still, the hurt inside him would not abate.

"Azeez," she said, whispering his name like a prayer,

turning to look at him, her lithe body angling itself beneath him like a bow. He was entrenched deep inside her, willing himself to pull out, willing himself to stop before he created new hurts, willing himself to close the vein that was still bleeding out.

He looked at her then, and the anger that had pushed him to use her like this, receded. He bent and took her mouth; only desire and his cold will was left now. She returned the kiss with equal fervor, with a desperation that tugged at his heart. But the kiss could not reach it.

He was so hard and deep inside her, her pleasure, her body, her mind, and even her strong will, they were all his in the moment as he wanted, she was his the way he wanted. Absolutely, where they only existed together. He could have happily died in that moment.

Reaching under her sensuous body, he filled his hands with her breasts and tweaked her nipples.

She immediately arched into him, losing all thought of that guttural request she had made. And he pulled out and thrust back.

The sound of that low moan she made in the back of her throat, the drag of his hips against hers, the shuddering in her long legs as he set an unrelenting rhythm, he let himself drown in all the sensations she created for him. She was perfect for him in every way, as he had always assumed, and he took her, slowly, deliciously, until the walls of her sex clamped him tight.

With every slow thrust, he plundered deeper inside her wet heat, for every coil of pleasure he took, he released the anger, the hurt inside him.

He searched inside for the last ounce of his control, kissed her spine and breathed the words into her. "I would have found a way, Nikhat, I would have protected you."

She gasped, but he didn't let her recover from his assault.

He found the center of her swollen heat and tweaked it between his fingers. Her climax broke out of her, and he rode on its waves. Her sex clenched him hard, the contractions of her muscles pushing him into his own release.

His orgasm reverberated through him, shattering him and rebuilding him at the same time. Still inside her, he clutched her to him for another weak, wavering moment, breathed in her scent, tasted her skin, reveled in the cocoon of her body.

She cared about him, he knew that. And she was back here; she had helped him see through the darkness into light. But the truth she had hidden, the sacrifice she had made, it unmanned him.

She was everything he had always thought she was, and by the same token, she had set herself out of his reach.

His first instinct was to bind her to him, to shackle her with his power until there was nowhere she could go, to leave her with no avenue except him.

And he fought black the cloud of his selfish desires, the thundering darkness of his heart, welcomed the chill that pervaded him as he finally made his decision.

To shackle her to him again when it was the very thing she had walked away from with complete certainty, it would break her. And he didn't want her like that.

He would agree to Ayaan's demands, do everything his brother had asked of him and he would do it the way it needed to be done.

His passionate nature rebelled at the thought of giving her up. His heart had never been denied, he had never learned control.

And to deny his heart what it wanted while doing his duty, that was to be his penance.

He picked up Nikhat and took her to the bathtub again. He turned on the water and washed her with the jasmine soap that she loved. He wiped her, wrapped her in a robe and carried her back to the bed.

And then he saw the tears in her beautiful brown eyes. She clasped his wrist and pressed her warm mouth to it as he pulled the covers over her.

"Sleep, *habeebi*," he whispered, and walked out of her suite without looking back.

His heart, finally, felt like a hard rock inside his chest. Something he had been struggling to achieve for six long years.

CHAPTER TWELVE

NIKHAT JERKED AWAKE from a fitful sleep and struggled to find her bearings. Her eyes were gritty. Sweat beaded her brow and her sheets were tangled around her hips. Unease weighed in her stomach and she turned to check the time. The little digital alarm clock said 5:00 a.m. Pushing the sheets away, she stepped down from the bed, lethargy making her slow.

Her body ached between her legs. Her abdomen was stiff, as if she had done a hundred push-ups, her arms hurt, too.

But it was more an exquisite soreness than any real pain and worth every bit.

For several seconds, she stood there, her vision dizzying, everything Azeez had said slamming back into her like pieces of a puzzle. The picture that emerged knocked the breath out of her.

I deserved the truth, Nikhat.

How did he know?

Her heart stuttered, struggling to keep up with her emotions. She changed into a caftan and leggings and grabbed a shawl to wrap around her torso.

The palace corridors were empty, eerie, and she couldn't shake off the impression that she was going to her doom.

No, she wasn't going to think like that. She shoved aside

the anxiety and hugged the relief that danced under that. Somehow, Azeez had learned the truth now. He was entitled to his anger.

But when his initial shock receded, he would surely understand why she had made the decision to leave him all those years ago. He had to. She wouldn't think about it any other way, she couldn't bear to.

Halting outside his suite's door, she sucked in a deep breath and clutched the edges of the shawl tight.

Everything inside her felt as if it hung in the balance, every minute of her life, every decision she had made falling away like sand sinking away under one's toes.

She pushed the door and struggled against the dazzling glare of light.

Approximately twenty men were inside the room, talking in small groups, some at laptops, some taking notes from Ayaan, she realized.

Had she been so lost in her own fears that she hadn't even heard a single voice?

Her heart pounded so loudly that for a few minutes all she could hear was the thundering beat of it in her ears. She felt her face heat as a sound escaped her mouth. One by one, the faces turned, the hushed whispers died down, shock and astonishment and even disapproval at her presence marring the strange faces.

For a dizzying second, Nikhat thought she would collapse under the weight of her own anxiety. Run, move, hide.

Her brain was issuing the standard flight responses, triggering fear in her, because she was standing outside the prince's wing, a wing that was forbidden to women, at the crack of dawn, her hair flowing behind her, clad in nothing but an old caftan and leggings, her eyes red-rimmed with the tears she had shed, her mouth and neck still bearing the evidence of his kisses.

And behind all of them, sitting in a gold-edged armchair covered in red velvet, his dark gaze calmly observing her, without anger, without any expression, really, was Azeez.

He looked forbidding, cold, a distant stranger, not at all the man she knew so intimately.

His gaze found hers the exact second hers found his. And still she did not turn around, she didn't fake confusion and flee as her rational mind was urging her to. She couldn't even look away from him.

She heard Ayaan's voice in a distant corner of her functioning mind, ordering them all to leave, she heard the room empty, she saw realization dawn on some faces that recognized her and curious disapproval on others that didn't. But it was all only on the periphery of her consciousness, almost as if it was happening to another poor deluded woman. Because, he, the dark Prince of Dahaar, he was at the center of her world, as he had always been.

She stepped in and closed the doors behind them. There was still no reaction in his face. He didn't blink, he didn't acknowledge her by the flicker of a muscle.

He only stared at her, an icy chill in his gaze, a remote set to his mouth, and that was when finally Nikhat began to worry.

She stopped when she neared him. Her shawl had fallen away long ago, leaving her in the thin cotton caftan separating her bare skin from his gaze.

And still, in the nothingness of his expression, in the riot of fear and worry that filled her, still, an electric charge danced between them.

There was nothing else to do but speak her mind, put her greatest fear into words. She stood in front of him, like his prisoner waiting for judgment.

"You have shown yourself to them," she said, standing awkwardly, her entire body trembling.

"As have you," he said, looking up at her, his gaze still inscrutable. "What will happen to your reputation, your dream, your clinic now?"

There was no threat in his words, implied or unsaid, but it was the utter lack of anything else that sent a shiver zig-zagging across her spine. It was unbearable that he freeze her out like this, unbearable to be in front of him and see a stranger.

A fierce churning began in her stomach, but she held it off.

No, he wouldn't, he couldn't be angry with her over this, it was not acceptable to her. She had to get them through this, he would understand why, he would see how much she loved him, how much it hurt to be away from him, how much a part of her permanently froze every time she left him.

This time she didn't want to go, she didn't want to break her heart again.

"You will not let any harm come to my reputation, or my dream."

With a soft grunt, he rose to his feet. The smile that curved his mouth chilled her to the core. It was full of such resignation that she would never forget it. "You trust me now? When you didn't trust me with the biggest truth of our lives?"

She clasped his hands, her own frightfully cold. He still did not sound angry and it was the very lack of that anger that scared her. Hours ago he had been angry when he made love to her. Now it felt as if there was just an icy dis-dain that she couldn't reach. "I did it for you, Azeez. They said…the chances of me conceiving were next to nil. That even if I went off my medication and tried, there would be no guarantees.

"That last trip to New York, the doctor performed a sur-gery immediately to remove some of the lesions.

"When I came back, I was so alone, so scared. I wanted to tell you, I wanted to howl. Then…my father said your coronation was imminent. And my heart shattered.

"I barely felt like a woman and to be your wife, to be the queen…But I still came to see you. And you—" tears spilled over her cheeks "—you were so excited. You said you couldn't wait to follow in your father's footsteps, that you couldn't wait to add your own stamp to the Al Sharif history, that you couldn't wait to create a legacy your heir, and your children, would want to carry forward.

"You needed a queen, you needed a wife who would give you sons, you needed a woman whose presence by your side would add strength to your rule, to your regime."

She hiccuped and wiped her hands over her cheeks. "You were vibrant, charming, a prince of the world. I…I already was nothing compared to you. It was an uphill battle for us both. Then to find that I might never conceive, that I was broken at the one thing you did need from me…I broke my own heart."

He grabbed her then, his fingers digging into her flesh. "Don't you dare call yourself broken."

"But I am. I spent my whole life seeing my father, an average aide to the royal family, disappointed again and again that he had no son. My mother knew the risks she was taking on her health and yet she had one child after another.

"An educated man like Richard…he knew all about my condition, he said he was fine with it…except when he decided he wanted children. It hurt so much to face that reality, to be denied my chance at happiness just because…God, if that had happened with you, if it was your resentment I would have to see every day, or even worse, if you had to take another wife for an heir, it would have killed me, it—"

"How dare you compare me to another man, how dare you extrapolate my feelings like I was an object of science? You don't know what I would have said or done. I was an honorable man. I would have loved you. I would have found—"

"You think I doubted your intentions?" It was her turn to shout. Her throat was raw, her eyes stung. But beneath it all, fear fisted her chest. "I trusted your word, your love, Azeez. I just couldn't put that choice in front of you. You would have hated me later, resented me for that choice. I couldn't bear the idea of it. I couldn't—"

He pulled her to him, his arm gentle around her. She felt his breath blow over her hair, felt the shudder that went through him. "You broke my heart, Nikhat, and you didn't even tell me the truth. You only thought of yourself."

His palms on her shoulders, he pushed her until he could look into her face. And the loss she saw there, it said everything he didn't say. "I love you, Azeez. I don't remember a moment of my life when I didn't."

"Do you know the meaning of the word? Even if I could understand why you didn't tell me all those years ago, what about the last few weeks? I bared everything to you, I let you see me at my darkest. All you did was protect yourself even as you made love with me. Was it your pride or your love that led you to hide the truth even then?"

"I'm sorry, Azeez. I am here now, I will be yours in any way you want me."

Any hint of softening she had seen vanished, leaving those eyes of his empty again. He had never felt more unattainable, more out of the reach of her heart. "Because now you *think* I'm as damaged as you are?"

She flinched, as if he had slapped her, as if he had called her very soul into question. And she realized what she had done. "I have never thought that, not for a second."

"You were right. If I had married you then, we would have destroyed each other with doubts and insecurities. And now, now there's nothing but bitterness of the past, Nikhat, nothing but broken and impossible dreams between us.

Maybe we never were worthy of each other."

He turned away from her, and his retreat was final, his withdrawal leaching away every ounce of warmth from the room. "You will leave the palace tomorrow. There will be a new obstetrician for Princess Zohra.

"No one will dare to talk about seeing you here, no one will dare point a finger in your family's direction. Not after the service you have done for us. Or they will face the crown's wrath.

"You will have your clinic. You will be back with your sisters. Thank you for everything you have done for me, Nikhat. I release you from your promise."

Only a few days had passed when Azeez learned that his parents were back in Dahaara, in the palace. And yet it felt as if it had been an eternity since he had taken the decision that would dictate the rest of his life.

That was already dictating it now.

Running both hands through his hair, he drew a shuddering breath as the guard announced his arrival in their private suite.

He pushed the doors open and breathed in relief as he saw Ayaan and Zohra also waiting. He had made the right decision. But he still needed Ayaan's support in this moment.

Grief, and pain and so much more that he couldn't sift through, it all rose inside him like the wave of a tsunami as he reached his mother.

And the pain he saw in her eyes, the aching hunger as she studied him, that she quickly covered up with a quiet dignity, the piercing hesitation in her smile, it lanced through him. God, how selfish he had been to rob her of this joy in the wake of everything she had borne, how foolish to rob himself of the warmth and understanding that stole through him.

Reaching for her hands, he tugged her up, tears now running down his cheeks freely. "Will you ever forgive me?"

A cry burst free from her mouth as she hugged him hard, her tears soaking through his tunic. Wrapping his arms around her, he held her through the wracking sobs that shook her fragile frame, whispered apologies and promises, and finally felt his world finding some kind of peace.

"I knew it. And after all these years, too... Do you see this, Zohra?" Ayaan quipped.

Her mouth wreathed in smiles, Zohra turned to him. "What?"

"He's still her favorite. I don't remember her hugging me that hard when I came back," he finally explained, and laughter rippled through the room.

Meeting his brother's gaze, Azeez offered a nod of thanks. He owed his brother everything and he was determined to spend his life taking every burden away from him.

This was how it had been, his family. It had been his strength, his joy. Amira was gone, but she would always have a place in their hearts. His gaze fell on Princess Zohra and the happiness he saw there.

And he felt heartened by it.

Even with his heart cold in his chest, he still had so much in the world to live for. He placed a kiss to the top of his mother's head, the scent of her calming him.

Wiping her hands over her cheeks, his mother smiled at him. "I have my sons back." She turned toward his father, the regal dignity that had always been her strength inching back into her shoulders. "More than I ever hoped for."

Turning toward his father, Azeez clasped his hands, saw the toll the past few years had taken on him. It was time for him to shoulder that burden, time for his father to rest. No matter that he was burying his own heart in the process.

When Azeez tried to speak, his father shook his head. "Let us leave the past where it is, Azeez. You're here now and prepared to aid your brother in serving Dahaar. That's all I've ever asked of you and Ayaan."

Azeez knelt in front of his king, the man who had taught him everything he knew, the man whom he had always looked up to. And felt the rightness of what he was about to say, knew that the woman he loved, would always love, would be proud of the man he had finally become again.

"If you and Mother will allow me, and if it's acceptable to Ayaan, I will spend the rest of my life doing what I was born to do, what you have prepared me for all my life, Father. I am ready to be king, ready to be Dahaar's servant for the rest of my life."

The shocked gasp from his mother, the unconventional and totally characteristic shout of joy from Princess Zohra, the sheen of tears in his father's eyes, the glint of shining pride in Ayaan's eyes as he reached Azeez and enfolded him in a tight hug, it flew through Azeez, lending him the strength he needed.

His father's simple yes reverberated in the room, and through the congratulations that followed the rest of the day, through the very joy and celebrations that began to pervade the palace, through his brother's concerned questions about Nikhat and him, Azeez kept a smile on his face and swallowed his own heartache.

CHAPTER THIRTEEN

NIKHAT WASHED HER hands at the sink in the attached bath-room of her clinic and grabbed a hand towel. Even though the building for her new clinic was air-conditioned and she had been back in Dahaar for a few weeks now, she wasn't used to the blistering heat of the day yet.

Making sure her hair stayed in her braid, she shied away from the mirror quickly, refusing to give in to the chasm of self-pity that was just waiting to drag her down.

She walked back into her consulting rooms. After almost a month, it still caught her breath every time she looked around and realized she was living her dream.

The new clinic was more than anything she had hoped for, in scope and breadth, thanks to the Princes of Dahaar.

It had been a month since she had left the palace...or rather she had been, with the utmost respect, kicked out. She had not let herself sit down for a minute, would not let herself stop even for a second.

When night came, she fell into exhausted sleep after being on her feet nonstop for twelve to thirteen hours. There were interviews she was conducting to find more qualified personnel—nurses, even midwives, not necessarily with the highest credentials, but the ones that most of the popu-lation in Dahaara trusted.

There was inventory to be organized and sorted every

day, medical supplies to be distributed. Not that any resource that she needed had been left out.

From an administrator for the clinic to oversee bureaucratic roadblocks she came across everywhere she turned, to a finance manager who had access and control over the fund that the royal family had set up for the clinic, from a twenty-year-old woman who was pursuing her degree in health care and was putting together educational material, pamphlets, even booklets to spread word about the clinic, to an elderly woman who brought lunches and coffee for the staff...every little detail had been sorted out.

All Nikhat needed was to finalize the candidates—which was proving the hardest, because qualified female doctors, ones that families would feel comfortable about sending the women of their families to, were hard to find.

She got a thrill every time she saw her name plaque outside the building. So what if, at the same time, she felt as if there was a hole in her chest? So what if she caught a spasm of such intense longing in the middle of the day that she thought she would never smile again?

The one thing she did wish she could do was tune out the world around her. It was hard enough, every second of every day, to push back the realization that he was just a few miles away in the palace and yet he had never been farther from her.

It was a month in which every day she felt her heart breaking again, in which Dahaar and its people had exploded with the news that Prince Azeez bin Rashid Al Sharif was alive and back in Dahaara.

Clutching the cold metal surface of her desk, she swallowed back the dizzying whirl of grief that rose through her. If she gave in to one tear, she was afraid she would not stop.

"Nikhat?"

She whirled around and saw Princess Zohra standing at

the entrance to her office, security guards hovering behind her. Drawing in a deep breath, Nikhat smiled. "Princess Zohra, please come in. You could have just summoned me to the palace if you—"

She caught herself as the princess dismissed the guards and closed the door behind her. Neither Princess Zohra, nor even Ayaan, could summon Nikhat to the palace.

Nikhat's name was not to be mentioned in the palace, not even her shadow was to be near it. That was the condition Azeez had laid out in front of his brother, Ayaan had told her, his face pinched.

Azeez Al Sharif did nothing in half measures. His rejection of her was as absolute as his love for her had been.

Even though still in her second trimester, Zohra was already big, and the strain showed on her fragile features. Hurrying to the other side of the desk, Nikhat pulled out a chair for her. Drawing a loud breath, Zohra shook her head.

"I would rather stand. All I do these days seems like sitting around, waiting for people to arrange my day, and my life.

"Now that King Malik and Queen Fatima are back, even my body is not my own. Queen Fatima is driving me crazy with her advice, her rituals, hovering over me. She won't let Azeez or me out of her sight, checking on us every few hours. Ayaan said he is beginning to feel like the ignored middle child.

"How I wish you were back there, Nikhat. The new ob-gyn is terrified of the queen and agrees to everything she proposes. Queen Fatima actually forbade me from visiting Siyaad, from seeing my sister and brother, and the stupid woman just nodded.

"I finally had to threaten Ayaan that I would leave for Siyaad and have the babies there unless he lets me see you here. I will come to you every few days, Nikhat. That way, you can check my progress and I get away from the blasted palace for a few hours. Ask your administrator to call my assistant. I'm sure my being your patient can be used to spread the word about the clinic. And if there's an emergency at the palace, that woman can tend to me. Will you still handle my delivery?"

Clutching Zohra's hands in hers, Nikhat smiled. "Of course, Princess Zohra. I—"

"Really, Nikhat. Can I just be Zohra with you?"

Smiling at her assertiveness, Nikhat nodded.

"That's great." She walked around her office and Nikhat had a feeling the princess was nowhere near done. Turning around, she studied Nikhat, her sharp gaze lingering over the dark shadows under her eyes. "You have no idea how thrilled I am that I don't have to be the queen. I know that Ayaan will still be extremely busy, but at least—"

Nikhat froze. "But…the coronation, it was supposed to be in a fortnight. Is it being postponed?"

Her gaze steady, Zohra shook her head. And Nikhat realized what Zohra was saying, what she had come to tell Nikhat. Blood rushed from her head, and spots danced in front of her eyes. The truth slammed into her from every side, she swayed where she stood. "He…" *Ya Allah*, it hurt to even speak his name. "He…is to be king?"

Reaching for her, Zohra steadied Nikhat. "Yes. They are making a statement tomorrow. The aides are all running around like crazy. Can you imagine? They have just over a week to find him—"

"A wife," Nikhat said, the word burning on her lips.

A prince needed a wife to be king.

Her mind whirled, the walls of the office she had cherished so much closing in on her. She couldn't continue to live in Dahaar and see the news of him with his wife, one who would give him sons, some unknown woman taking everything Nikhat wanted.

It was unbearable.

"If you are thinking of just running away again, believe me, Nikhat, it won't help."

Nikhat turned around, astonished at how well Zohra could read her mind. "What do I do, Zohra? I broke my own heart last time. I…I can't give him what he needs."

"I don't believe the man I've come to know the last few weeks, everything I've learned about what he has been through, he…gives his heart lightly, nor will he resent you for what you can't change. You reached through to him when not even his parents and brother could, Nikhat. Doesn't that tell you something?"

"You know?"

Her hands resting on her belly, Zohra nodded. "Ayaan told me after I pestered him about you and Azeez.

"I can't imagine what you must have felt when you learned about your condition. I can't imagine feeling like I couldn't be everything Ayaan needed me to be. But how it will dictate your life, that's up to you."

There was no sympathy or comfort in Zohra's voice. Only cold hard facts. Maybe if she had had a friend like this before, maybe if she had confided in someone…Nikhat smiled through the sheen of tears gathering in her eyes, appreciating Zohra's coming all the way. "Thank you, Zohra."

"I do feel safe in your hands. But I didn't come for you. I came for him."

"For Azeez?"

"I understand now why it killed Ayaan to see Azeez like that, why he was prepared to do anything for his brother.

"Because Azeez would too.

"He agreed to everything Ayaan set in front of him, he

even agreed to bear your presence, despite his pride, so that I would feel better, didn't he? I don't like the look that has come back into his eyes. He is my brother, too, now, and my king. He has my loyalty, and my love.

"But if you go near him, make sure you know your mind, Nikhat. Because it's not his acceptance you're craving, is it?"

With that parting shot, Zohra left, leaving Nikhat reeling under the weight of her words. No one had ever spoken to her like that, ever cut through the pain she had surrounded herself with, so effectively.

For the rest of the afternoon, Nikhat went through her duties like an automaton. She visited a couple of patients in their homes, went through the inventory and finally went home.

Her sisters' laughter and conversation surrounded her with its usual warmth yet she felt as if she was removed from it all, a deep freeze surrounding her heart.

A strange sort of fever gripped her, and yet fear held her back. She went in search of her father, the only choice left to her slowly gaining power inside her head. And with that came anger, too, and the strength to speak her mind.

She found him standing on the balcony, looking out into the streets of Dahaara.

He turned as she approached, frowning. "Nikhat? Is something wrong?"

She glared at him, the haunting desperation in her finding a target. Years of pain coated her cutting words, the freedom of finally making a decision lending her the strength to lash out. "You knew he's going to be king. And yet you didn't say a word. Are you so ashamed of me? Do I mean nothing to you?"

His mouth compressed, he blanched and she thought he would walk away without a word. But she wouldn't let him.

Instead, he covered her hand with his. And tears gathered in her throat. "I have never wanted this grief for you, Nikhat."

"No, all you wanted was for me to be average and traditional, but I'm not, Father."

"You think I don't know that?" He sighed deeply, something stark in his gaze. "I never quite learned how to protect you."

Her gaze flew to him. "What are you talking about?"

"I know you blame me for your mother's death. But I never wanted a son at the cost of her life, Nikhat. She did. She was obsessed with it, weaved dreams about what I wanted."

Just as Nikhat had done. She sagged against the wall. She always thought that it had been her father who had wanted a son. And yet thinking back, he had never actually said that. "Why didn't you ever tell me?"

Her father stared ahead and she instantly realized he was not comfortable talking about this. And yet he was making the effort. "You were twelve when she died, Nikhat. You were already grieving, taking on so many duties around the house. And later, I didn't want to taint your memory of her.

"Why would I feel the need for a son when I had you, when in every way that mattered, you always helped me as much as you could?"

Shock reverberating through her, Nikhat shook her head. Lies, they had to be lies. But having lived away for so long, she had forgotten what a rigid, traditional man her father was. Had she expected him to be different just as she was now?

Clutching her hand tight between his, he met her gaze. And the pride and love she saw in those brown eyes that she had inherited, swept through her. "From the moment you were born, you were this bundle of wonder, Nikhat, unlike anything I had ever expected in a daughter.

"Like every other man in Dahaar, I thought you had very less consequence for me. I loved you as I do every one of your sisters, but you...you were a revelation.

"As you grew older, I had no idea what I would do with you, how to channel your intelligence, your thirst for more than I could provide. I was both afraid and so proud when King Malik commanded that you be educated by Princess Amira's side.

"I despaired of how I would protect you, your happiness from the world, from your own expectations..." He exhaled a long breath. "And from Prince Azeez.

"As your father, that was my foremost duty to you, Nikhat. To protect you.

"When you learned of your condition, I was terrified of what you would do."

"You knew?"

"Of course I knew. I read every report, and it broke my heart. Once again, I was afraid of what kind of future you would have in Dahaar. But you shocked me with your strength. And suddenly, I saw that you had the perfect solution. You were destined for greater things, and Dahaar and I, we would do nothing but curtail you. Prince Azeez would bring nothing but pain to you.

"So I insisted you not return. For your own good and for your sisters'."

He had given her so much thought and she...she had thought him hard-hearted, uncaring about anything but tradition. A tear rolled down her cheek. It was apparently the day she had to walk through fire. "I had a good life in New York, Father. But I needed you and my sisters, too."

"Forgive me for not realizing that, Nikhat. When you came back and when I heard the rumors, I thought history was repeating itself. And your sisters, they are not like you."

Her heart bursting, Nikhat hugged him hard, even as she felt him stiffen against her. He was not used to such blatant gestures or displays of emotion. He had never been, would never be.

And she had to accept him this way, accept that he had loved her in his own way, and had tried to protect her the only way he knew.

This was why he hadn't met her eyes since she had returned from the palace, why he had banned her sisters from voicing their incessant questions about the coronation.

And that small fact gave her a fierce strength.

She pulled back, her heart racing faster and faster. She smiled at him as he looked at her quietly. "I have to go to him, Father. I have to show him my heart. I have to hope that he will accept my love, see that I'm ready for him."

That old intractability swept into his gaze, but this time she saw it for his concern. His shoulders a tight line, he nodded. "Are you ready for the consequences, Nikhat?"

Nikhat nodded, battling the fear that knotted her stomach.

Had Azeez already made his decision that last night they had spent together? Was that why he had been so ferociously cruel with her? She hadn't realized she had presented him with a choice, that she had only wanted him if he could be anyone but himself; but the king.

Her love or his duty?

And after everything he had gone through to find himself again…

She had to believe that he still loved her. She couldn't bear to think of a future without him now. And if he did love her…if she wanted to share her life with Azeez, she would have to face the fact every day that she might never have children. Everyone would question her eligibility, a whole nation would wonder about her inability to conceive.

But he…he would never resent her. She had loved him before there had been guilt and shadows in his eyes and she loved the honorable man he was now. To imply that he didn't feel the same for her was calling into question his very honor, his very nature, the very thing that made him Azeez Al Sharif.

All along, she had thought she had accepted her condition, she had thought she had forged herself a life, went after her dreams despite it.

But she had robbed herself of her biggest happiness, run far from the one man she had loved more than life itself. Her strength had been nothing but a mirage, an illusion.

For the first time in her life, she felt as if she was ready to choose her own happiness, as if she was worthy of the man she loved.

"I've always been his, Father."

Ten more days.

There were ten more days before his coronation and he didn't know how long before he took a wife. He had met a couple of the "eligible candidates" this morning. He couldn't remember their names, much less their faces.

Nodding at his mother and her aides, he had said any one of them was acceptable to him. He knew, in the back of his mind, that he was being more than cruel to the woman in question. None of this was her fault. But seeing them was all he could manage before his gut churned with a vicious force.

None of them was the woman he wanted with every breath in him.

They knew what they were getting into, he reassured

himself, walking back into his bedchamber and dismissing his three assistants and two aides with one command.

His physiotherapist lingered, a flash of anxiety on the younger man's face. Azeez signaled for him to leave, too, even knowing that he couldn't afford to miss any sessions, not the night before the public statement was going to be made by his father.

He walked to the middle of the room and tried to move his hip joint in the way Nikhat had taught him.

But instead of that, all he could see was her face. Her lush mouth pinched, her heart in her eyes, breaking, shattering, her body gathered into a tight mass as if she braced herself against him, against his cruel words.

The chasm of yearning in his gut, it felt as wide open as ever and just as painful. He heard the door open behind him and barked an order at whoever dared to come inside after he had banished them all.

Silence met his command. And then he felt it. The way the hairs on his neck stood up, the hint of evening breeze that reached his nostrils coated with jasmine...

There was no jasmine in the courtyards of the Dahaaran palace.

He turned around just as she reached him. Her arms wound around her midriff, her face turned up toward him, she was warmth, she was light, she was the most beautiful, the most courageous woman he had ever seen in the world.

And his heart hurt to look at her and not reach for her.

He stepped back from her, ruthlessly cutting away the thread of hope that flagged within. "Who do I have to punish for letting you in here?"

She didn't answer. Only continued to stare at him—hungrily, greedily, as if she owned him. And she did, she had done for so many years.

"Nikhat?"

Blinking, she met his gaze. "Zohra."

"Ah...of course. I have never met a more stubborn woman, except perhaps you. I have no idea how Ayaan puts up with her." He turned away from her, her wind-kissed hair, the dark shadows under her eyes, challenging his very will. "Why are you here, Nikhat?"

"Will you forgive me, Azeez?"

Nikhat shivered, wondering if she'd died a thousand little deaths in the few seconds that Azeez took to respond. When he turned around, there was no softening of the hard planes of his face, no fire in his empty gaze. He looked tired, drawn, as if he was made of ice and cold rather than the heat and blaze of the desert.

And she realized, she had done this to him.

There was no power in it, only shame. She had truly not been worthy of him until now. She shoved away the clamor of fear that said she had lost him forever, that voice of despair that threatened to pull her under. If she lost him now...

Reaching into the pocket of her coat, she pulled out the box Ayaan had handed her just a few minutes ago, before he had enfolded her in a hug that sent tears to her eyes. She wished she felt half his confidence.

The long velvet case was soft in her hand. Her fingers shaking, it took her what felt like an eternity to open the jeweled clasp. He still didn't say a word.

But now, now Nikhat could feel the tension coil around them, as if someone had left a live wire around them, fizzing, crackling with expectations, and hope and love.

Her jaw fell as she saw the two rubies—one big, sitting in a stark setting, and the relatively smaller one set in twinkling diamonds. She almost lost her nerve then. She looked up to see Azeez eye the rings, saw the moment realization dawned on him.

His jaw tightened, but the fire in his eyes, she knew that fire. "Be very careful about what you're going to say, *ya habeebiti*." Instead of scaring her, however, the low warning note in his words stirred her, stroking her heart, her skin, the very core of her.

Clasping his hands, she looked up at him. "I'm sorry for running away from your love. I'm sorry for not trusting you enough. I thought my condition made me unworthy of you, but it was my fear, my doubt of your love and my own." She had to breathe to speak past the lump in her throat. "I know that you'll protect me from the world, from everyone, even my own insecurities. And I need you, Azeez, I need the joy you bring to my life. I'm ready to be your wife, Azeez, I'm finally ready to be your queen."

The fingers that tilted her chin up were shaking, and when she met his gaze, the love that glimmered in those dark depths shook her from within. "It killed me to send you away, Nikhat." A shudder racked his powerful frame and she hugged him harder, tighter, realizing it was fear. "It wrecked me to tear out my own heart like that, *habeeba*. But you, your magnificent strength, your innate duty, you left me no choice. Realizing that I was in love with you again, whilst also realizing, in that same moment, the man I *needed* to be, it tore me apart. But I couldn't ask you to bear this for me. Not when you made the choice once to walk away from this very fate."

"No. Not from you." Pressing her cheek to his chest, she curled around him, feeling the hard muscles, learning him. He was her home, her everything. "I understand now, Azeez. And I'm so sorry I took so long to realize it. I wish—"

Clasping her cheek, he pressed a fierce kiss to her mouth that shook her very soul. The scent and taste of him seeped into her, invigorating her, filling her with a dizzying joy that had her shivering.

With a hard grip, he tugged her against him, until there was nothing to look at but his beautiful, proud face. "I've never doubted your strength, Nikhat. Your strength in the face of everything you went through, your sense of purpose in everything you have accomplished, it made me realize what I needed to do.

"You showed me I couldn't walk away from my destiny. And I've only ever wanted it with you by my side, *habeeba*."

Smiling through her tears, she plucked the ring out of the case and slid it onto his finger. They had been made for each other, they had both been through fire and emerged to find each other again. "You are the most honorable, most courageous man I've ever met and you are mine."

He clasped her cheek and kissed her, and Nikhat melted into his embrace. "Always," he said, his gaze shining. He pushed the ruby ring onto her finger and kissed her hand, his heart, his love shining in his eyes. "You complete me, Nikhat. You always have. I don't need an heir, I don't need anything in the world, if you are by my side. Do you understand?"

Nikhat nodded, her heart bursting to full with joy, and fierce determination.

EPILOGUE

Seven months later...

THE SOUNDS OF infants crying, loud and wailing, as he pushed the door of his suite had the king of Dahaar doing a double take and checking he had, indeed, entered his own royal chambers.

Confirming that these were indeed his chambers, he closed the doors behind him and leaned against them. The sight that greeted him stole his breath.

His queen, Dr. Nikhat Salima Zakhari Al Sharif, was kneeling on a centuries-old rug, cooing to the little infant with jet-black hair.

The baby cooed at her in return, his toothless mouth splitting into a grin. She changed his diaper, scrunched her nose and turned to his identical twin, who instantly kicked his legs and bestowed a matching smile on her.

"You know, instead of standing there, smiling at us, you could come here and maybe help, Your Highness?"

Laughing, Azeez pushed off the door and reached her.

He slowly sank to the floor, next to her, and picked up the first one.

His nephew didn't smile at him as he did at his wife. He made a note to have his assistant block some time every week—even an hour—that he could spend with them.

Nikhat was always helping out Zohra anyway, in addition to her clinic and her royal duties. His wife, he had discovered, was a bundle of energy, always on the go. Having been so close to his sister and the palace, there wasn't a thing she didn't know. Even his mother hadn't been able to find fault with her. "Which one is this—Rafiq or Tariq?"

Shaking her head, Nikhat picked up the second infant. "How can you not tell? That's Rafiq, older by a whole three minutes, and he totally looks like Zohra. He has her stubbornness, her temper."

Azeez studied him and stole a look at the other one, seeing nothing but identical jet-black eyes like his own and not Ayaan's copper-hued ones, jet-black hair and chubby cheeks.

She cuddled Tariq, and made unintelligible noises. Azeez's breath stuck in his throat. His wife was a natural with babies, a fact Zohra seemed to be eternally grateful for, as she herself was struggling with postpartum depression.

Azeez had been so afraid for Nikhat the first few weeks after Zohra had delivered the twins almost three weeks early. She had been unable to sleep, always going over to see them, wanting to help Zohra, wanting to make sure the twins were okay. His heart had turned into a tight fist in his chest as he waited and watched, hoping and praying that Zohra, even if completely justified, didn't push Nikhat away, or get possessive about her sons. He needn't have worried.

Zohra's heart, it seemed, was as big as her smile. She had welcomed Nikhat with open arms, had leaned on her for real help, overwhelmed by her still-suffering health and her loud, premature-born sons. "Whereas Tariq here is his father's son. He's rarely, if ever, fussy, and sleeps like a dream. Your mother said Ayaan was like that as a baby."

"I guess she told you I was a terror, even as a baby."
Azeez mock frowned and rubbed his nose in Rafiq's fleshy
tummy. Little fingers instantly grabbed his hair and tugged
hard.

She laughed and they spent a few more minutes playing with his nephews. Once they began to yawn, he followed her to the matching cribs she insisted on having in
the second bedroom of their suite. An exact replica of the
ones in Ayaan and Zohra's bedchamber.

*I want to be a real aunt, Azeez, and not just one that buys
toys or plays with them for a few minutes. I want to help her.*

When he had expressed concern about Zohra, she had
smiled at him, tears shimmering in her eyes.

*Zohra said growing up, she'd always had only one par-
ent—either her mother or father—she's glad that her little
boys get two sets instead.*

Swallowing away the sudden knot in his throat, Azeez
followed her lead and laid down Rafiq. He waited as she
fussed a little more, and neatly wrapped them up until they
were snug.

Sighing, she stepped back and he instantly pulled her
tight against him. The scent of her skin both calmed and
aroused him, and he grew instantly hard.

She turned her head so that he could nuzzle into her
neck and with a groan, he grasped her hips and pulled her
into him. "I haven't seen you in a week, wife. I don't want
to share you tonight with these rogues."

"Ayaan is back from Siyaad. I thought it would be nice
if they could have some quiet. And between Zohra and me
and your mother, we don't want to leave the children overnight with nannies unless absolutely necessary."

Grabbing his hair, she angled her head and kissed him.
He sucked her tongue into his mouth, laved her lower lip,
waves of desire as intense as that first time, rolling through

him like a fierce hurricane. "The rogues won't be up for two hours, hopefully," she breathed into his mouth. She turned on the baby monitors before closing the door behind her.

"How did the interviews go in New York for new doctors?" he asked as they reached their own bedchamber. He filled his hands with her lush breasts, the graze of her hard nipples against his palms sending him into a fever. He would suckle them until she made those little noises in the back of her throat, make her climax until she was sobbing his name again.

His name on her lips when they made love, her body all wrapped up around him when they woke, the way she met his gaze across a crowded room and smiled at him, the way she had burrowed into him and sobbed after delivering the twins, *ya Allah*, he loved everything about this woman.

She mumbled some answer, shedding her top first and then peeling off her leggings, revealing long, toned thighs that sent blood rushing from his head. They were too eager, too desperate for each other to indulge in foreplay. On his next breath, she pushed him onto the bed and straddled him.

Nothing mattered but the pursuit of release, of moving inside her, of pushing her toward her own climax.

They came together in a rush of heat and pleasure. He gathered her against him and kissed her forehead, the scent of sweat and sex and her filling his nostrils.

She drew maddening circles on his chest and he caught her hands in his. He kissed each finger, her palm, the underside of her wrist, trying to soothe her, waiting for her to open up and tell him what was on her mind.

Unlike him, she never said everything that came into her head instantly, her first impulse was to worry about it herself, as she had done for so many years. But they had learned each other now. She knew he would wait, as much as he could, and he knew she would come to him, if not as soon as he wanted.

She finally met his gaze, and his breath caught again at the vulnerability in those eyes, the trust she showed him, the love she had for him. "I saw some fertility specialists when I was in New York."

His first instinct was hurt that she hadn't told him. But he fought the sensation. He pressed his mouth to her temple, ran his hand over the dip of her belly and nudged her even closer to him. That he could not take away this pain from her was the most agonizing fact of his own life. He tugged her chin up. "My mother will never again ask you about this, *ever*. Do you understand?"

You're a natural mother, Nikhat. Dahaar is waiting for its next crown prince.

A tear rolled out of the corner of her eye and his heart ached. She laced her fingers with his and kissed his hand. "It was not her fault, Azeez. We should have told her. They are all going to ask."

"I have had a discussion with my father and Ayaan. Once Zohra is a little better, we will declare Rafiq my heir, announce him the Crown Prince. If I could bear this pain for you, I would, *habeebiti*. Forgive me for wanting you, for being selfish enough to love you. That you face this question because of me—"

Her finger landed on his lips, her eyes glittering like rare gems. "It's never far from my mind, Azeez. I had resigned to spend my life alone. You're my strength, Azeez, my happiness. Tell me you believe that."

"I do."

She scrubbed her cheeks and rubbed her nose against his. "I went through a few more tests. The plan is to stop my medication and just see what—"

He sat up in such a sudden movement that his hip throbbed. "No."

His answer resonated in the silence between them. Turning around, he lay down on his side and kissed her hard. The image of her writhing in pain, he never wanted to see that again. "I don't want a child at the cost of your pain, Nikhat. This point is nonnegotiable."

"We don't know that it is even possible, Azeez. I have been on this medication for so long, it would be a good idea to just see how my body would react to other kinds." Clasping his cheek, she turned him so he was looking at her.

A shiver traveled down his spine. Even after the attack, he had never been as scared as the night she had cried after Zohra had delivered.

"I want to try this for myself."

He saw the resolve in her eyes and relented. "Six months."

She rolled her eyes and pouted. "It takes even an average couple six months to conceive."

"We are not average." He loved the gleam in her eyes when she tried hard not to laugh. "We are the king and queen of Dahaar. Normal laws of procreation don't apply to us."

Looping her arms around him, she giggled against him, her soft body rubbing against him making him hard all over again. "Yes, Your Highness. You have magical sperm that will find my mythical eggs no matter where they are hidden, and penetrate them…"

Laughing, she fell onto his lap, her mouth curved wide, tears rolling down her cheeks.

He captured her lips with his, taking her smiles and her pain. She sobered up and clung to him, her body trembling. Drawing in a deep breath, he held her hard. "You are my life, *ya habeebiti*, my pride, my power, my laughter, my joy.

"One year, Nikhat. That's all I will give you. I will not let this destroy you. I will lose the very will you brought me back if this takes you away from me. Do you understand?"

Nikhat gazed into the eyes of the most beautiful, the most honorable man she had ever seen. His embrace, his heart, his love, there wasn't a day that went by that she didn't wonder at the miracle that it was all hers. She nodded and smiled. "I'm strong enough for this, Azeez. With you by my side, I'm strong enough for anything." She lost herself in his kiss, basking in his love.

Whatever the future might bring, she had his heart and she would hold on to it.

* * * * *

ROMANCE

MEDICAL

Mills & Boon® Large Print
November 2014

ROMANCE

Christakis's Rebellious Wife	Lynne Graham
At No Man's Command	Melanie Milburne
Carrying the Sheikh's Heir	Lynn Raye Harris
Bound by the Italian's Contract	Janette Kenny
Dante's Unexpected Legacy	Catherine George
A Deal with Demakis	Tara Pammi
The Ultimate Playboy	Maya Blake
Her Irresistible Protector	Michelle Douglas
The Maverick Millionaire	Alison Roberts
The Return of the Rebel	Jennifer Faye
The Tycoon and the Wedding Planner	Kandy Shepherd

HISTORICAL

A Lady of Notoriety	Diane Gaston
The Scarlet Gown	Sarah Mallory
Safe in the Earl's Arms	Liz Tyner
Betrayed, Betrothed and Bedded	Juliet Landon
Castle of the Wolf	Margaret Moore

MEDICAL

200 Harley Street: The Proud Italian	Alison Roberts
200 Harley Street: American Surgeon in London	Lynne Marshall
A Mother's Secret	Scarlet Wilson
Return of Dr Maguire	Judy Campbell
Saving His Little Miracle	Jennifer Taylor
Heatherdale's Shy Nurse	Abigail Gordon

Mills & Boon® Hardback
December 2014

ROMANCE

Taken Over by the Billionaire	Miranda Lee
Christmas in Da Conti's Bed	Sharon Kendrick
His for Revenge	Caitlin Crews
A Rule Worth Breaking	Maggie Cox
What The Greek Wants Most	Maya Blake
The Magnate's Manifesto	Jennifer Hayward
To Claim His Heir by Christmas	Victoria Parker
Heiress's Defiance	Lynn Raye Harris
Nine Month Countdown	Leah Ashton
Bridesmaid with Attitude	Christy McKellen
An Offer She Can't Refuse	Shoma Narayanan
Breaking the Boss's Rules	Nina Milne
Snowbound Surprise for the Billionaire	Michelle Douglas
Christmas Where They Belong	Marion Lennox
Meet Me Under the Mistletoe	Cara Colter
A Diamond in Her Stocking	Kandy Shepherd
Falling for Dr December	Susanne Hampton
Snowbound with the Surgeon	Annie Claydon

MEDICAL

Midwife's Christmas Proposal	Fiona McArthur
Midwife's Mistletoe Baby	Fiona McArthur
A Baby on Her Christmas List	Louisa George
A Family This Christmas	Sue MacKay

Mills & Boon® Large Print
December 2014

ROMANCE

Zarif's Convenient Queen	Lynne Graham
Uncovering Her Nine Month Secret	Jennie Lucas
His Forbidden Diamond	Susan Stephens
Undone by the Sultan's Touch	Caitlin Crews
The Argentinian's Demand	Cathy Williams
Taming the Notorious Sicilian	Michelle Smart
The Ultimate Seduction	Dani Collins
The Rebel and the Heiress	Michelle Douglas
Not Just a Convenient Marriage	Lucy Gordon
A Groom Worth Waiting For	Sophie Pembroke
Crown Prince, Pregnant Bride	Kate Hardy

HISTORICAL

Beguiled by Her Betrayer	Louise Allen
The Rake's Ruined Lady	Mary Brendan
The Viscount's Frozen Heart	Elizabeth Beacon
Mary and the Marquis	Janice Preston
Templar Knight, Forbidden Bride	Lynna Banning

MEDICAL

200 Harley Street: The Soldier Prince	Kate Hardy
200 Harley Street: The Enigmatic Surgeon	Annie Claydon
A Father for Her Baby	Sue MacKay
The Midwife's Son	Sue MacKay
Back in Her Husband's Arms	Susanne Hampton
Wedding at Sunday Creek	Leah Martyn

1114 GEN STD LP